ENAMORED

SUSAN SCOTT SHELLEY

❀ Created with Vellum

CHAPTER ONE

LIAM

From his position in the ballpark's tunnel, Liam York adjusted the head of his shark costume and made a last-minute check on his custom-made skateboard. He'd worked hard at entertaining the crowd during the previous six innings, but for the seventh inning stretch of the last game of Spring Training, he had something special prepared for the crowd. Something he hadn't discussed with the members of the Riptide. Or management for that matter. But wasn't surprise the very spirit of April Fool's Day?

Gaze fixed on the green field and the players, he mentally ran through his routine. Skateboarding in the outfield while attached to an ATV via a rope would be awesome. Adding in some jumps and backflips would hopefully give the effect that Fin the Shark was water-skiing. He'd painted his skateboard a bright red and had a friend attach snowboard bindings so the board would stay secured to his feet.

Defending the title of League's Best Mascot took a lot of creativity and he intended to start off the season with a bang. Perfecting the stunt here, before he broke it out for the home crowd, made the most sense.

Sweat rolled down his face and chest and coated his limbs, but he couldn't do anything about it. The shark costume covered every inch of his body and the only relief came from the mesh patch of the shark mouth that doubled as his means of seeing and breathing. Still, it was comfortable. The arms and legs allowed flexibility and mobility, even if he was roasting inside the fabric thanks to the nearly triple-digit temperature baking the ball field. Nothing compared to the dry Arizona heat. He couldn't wait to get home to L.A. Not that the temperatures would be much better there.

The driver of the ATV twisted to face him. "That's the Bolts' last out. You ready to take the field?"

Liam grinned. "I was born ready."

That part was true enough. Growing up as the son of the mascot, and seeing the smiles his dad had brought to fans, players, and kids they'd visit in the hospital, Liam had wanted nothing more than to follow in his footsteps. After his dad had retired a few years ago, he'd been given his chance. As far as he was concerned, he had the best job in the world and was lucky enough to appreciate it.

He held tight to the rope as the ATV rumbled onto the field. The crowd, a mix of both Riptide and Bolts fans, roared as Fin the Shark came into view. He grinned as the board's wheels rolled through the grass. Waving to the crowd, he gripped the rope in his other hand and prepared for his first jump.

Backflips and other gymnastics were part of his repertoire. Liam crouched and then leaped, throwing his body backward. Blue sky and then the green grass filled his vision, and he squeezed the rope as he stuck the landing. The board stayed attached to his feet.

Success.

The roar of the crowd drowned out his thundering heartbeat. Adjusting his grip on the rope, he waved at a little boy in the first row who wore a T-shirt with a cartoonized version of Fin. Having his own fans was the coolest thing ever.

The driver gave him a thumbs-up and increased the speed as he continued around the field. They passed the Riptide dugout and his buddies on the team called out things he couldn't make out over the ATV's engine but he caught sight of Slade and Dom's grins. The team held the lead—seven runs to the Bolt's goose egg. Barring any huge mistakes, they had the win in the bag. After the game and into the night would be filled with celebration. His successful stunt would contribute to heightening the party.

The ATV headed for center field. Liam readied for one last jump. Instead of a simple backflip, he debated going for three in a row. He had enough space. And that feat might make the sports networks' highlight reels, might bring in more attention and then donations to his partnership with the children's charity.

He waved to the crowd again, then launched his body into the air.

One flip down.

Two down.

Three.

Mid-launch, the rope pulled to the left and slipped from his grasp. The world turned upside down. His stomach lurched and his heart slammed into his throat. He came down hard, landing upright on the board, and then careened toward the outfield wall. Adrenaline pumped through his blood. He waved his arms—anything to slow him down—but the wall came fast. His body slammed into the unforgiving padded barrier. Pain bloomed in his ankle and knee and the air rushed out of his lungs. The ground rushed up to meet him, finally ending his flight.

He lay, gasping, staring at the sky. The pain in his leg increased into intense bursts of agony. Silence flooded his ears. The only time the ballpark was completely still was during an on-field injury or when it was empty. He raised his head, lifted one arm...

"Liam!" Slade's voice reached him a second before his best friend knelt beside him. "What the hell? Are you okay?"

"Ugh." He didn't know. Didn't think so. But damn, he'd make the highlight reel all right—as a blooper. Not a good start to the season.

"Don't move." Andy Stevens, one of the team's physicians, crouched by his other side and released the skateboard's bindings. "Let me check you over."

The team's trainers joined Andy and other members of the Riptide gathered around Slade, some bending to offer encouragement and others looking on. Liam grimaced as Andy inspected his ankle. The touches weren't helping him feel better at all. He focused on Slade. The first baseman was one of the best power hitters in the league, but more than that, he was Liam's roommate and best friend. Slade smiled and shook his head. "That was some stunt you pulled."

"I try."

Andy asked him if he hit his head, what had happened, if he felt pain anywhere. Being evaluated while still wearing his shark costume, he felt a little ridiculous. Finally, the doctor motioned for the players and staff to step back. "Can you stand? We need to get you into the training room and out of that costume for a proper evaluation."

Slade propped him up on one side and Dom joined on the other. Supporting his weight, they lifted him to standing. Cheers and applause rang out from the crowd. He took a tentative step on his left leg and his ankle screamed in protest.

"Shit. That's not happening." At least the shark head hid

his face from the crowd. He didn't want to let on how bad he felt.

Dom nodded and adjusted his grip, accepted more of Liam's weight. "Don't worry. We've got you."

Leaning on his friends, Liam kept his gaze down, focusing on the grass and then the warning track during the slow hobble toward the dugout. Taking another tumble would be awful. Dom and Slade were all but carrying him.

"I'm sure you didn't hurt yourself too bad." Slade's cheerful optimism helped even as the lines fanning from his eyes deepened, giving away his concern. "You didn't feel anything snap, right?"

"Right. Except maybe my pride."

"Pride? You don't have pride, you're a mascot." Dom teased, giving his shoulder a squeeze. "You pulled off one ballsy stunt even if it didn't end the right way. You never let things get you down, so don't start now."

"Yeah, but—"

"No buts." Dom guided them to the steps leading into the dugout. "Just relax and let Andy check you out. We'll probably be laughing about this on the flight home tonight."

Liam bit his lip against the throbbing pain. The guys were probably right. Nothing bad would happen to him, not at the start of the season.

He had too much riding on it.

———

April Fools' Day.

Shit. Fate turned the surprise around on him, like a sick curse.

Less than twenty-four hours after the accident, Liam sat on a chair in front of the dugout in the Riptide's nearly empty stadium, wanting to be anywhere else. He glared at his metal crutches gleaming in the harsh sunlight and then the cast on his left foot. Stupid injury.

A fractured ankle meant six weeks or more for the bone to heal, followed by as many weeks of physical therapy as necessary to rebuild his strength and mobility. He would be stuck riding the proverbial bench for at least the first half of the season. But Andy had warned him full healing could take six months to as much as a year. Predicting ankles was a funny business.

From where Liam was sitting, he didn't see a damn thing funny. What he *did* see were five hopefuls on the sun-drenched ball field vying for his job.

Team management couldn't afford to lose the entertainment value that Liam brought to Fin the Shark, with the flips and daredevil activities, so they were replacing him.

And he was expected to help select and also train the new Fin.

Freaking fantastic. He scuffed his sneaker through the warning track's deep red-brown dirt, feeling as low as the dust kicked up by his movement.

"Hey, Liam." Slade strolled through the dugout. Hands tucked into his back pockets, he ascended the steps and then leaned against the fence at Liam's back. "Stop snarling. People are going to think you broke your funny bone too."

Liam snorted and shifted his crutches away from Slade's sneaker. "What are you doing here? I figured you'd spend your last weekend of freedom far away from the field."

"What can I say? I missed you." Slade shot him a grin. "You looked so down when I dropped you off earlier. So, since you're here, being miserable, I figured I'd come back and be miserable too."

Having his friend there for support helped a lot, but still…

the way Slade expected happiness and sunshine was too much. "I can't help that I'm not excited about the team bringing in someone to replace me."

Slade rolled his eyes. They'd had this discussion a ton of times since he'd received both the diagnosis and the team's plan last night. "Not *replace*. *Help out* until you get back to normal. Although, *normal* is a stretch for you."

Liam fought his first smile since the injuries had happened. "Thanks."

"Seriously, no one's as good as you. No other mascots can do the flips or stunts that you do. You have nothing to worry about."

Liam shaded his eyes and shrugged. One injury could change everything in an instant. After all, that was how his dad had scored the mascot job twenty years earlier, filling in after the original mascot had suffered a broken back. "This job means everything, man. I can't lose it. Do you know how many visits to Children's Hospital I have lined up already? And we're partnering with the Wishes Foundation again this season. I'm not giving up those appearances. Those kids need *me*, not some fill-in who doesn't understand how important those visits really are. I don't care if I have to steal my costume to be there."

"Please don't actually steal the costume. I can't be an accessory to the crime. It wouldn't look good for my contract negotiations."

"Well, someone has to drive the getaway car. I can't maneuver too well on my own yet." Liam grinned at Slade, grateful for his partner in crime's presence. His friend had always been there for him, through thick and thin and everything in between.

Laughing, Slade shook his head. "Dude, relax. This sucks right now, but the team owes you a lot for turning Fin into the money-making star that he is. They aren't going to forget about you."

"Maybe." He scanned the field. The sight of all the vigorous mascot wannabes his heart sank into his cast.

"Smile, damn it. You can't mope. Or at least you can't let them see you moping. You're still the face of Fin and if you really want to keep your job, show management your sense of humor is intact." Slade pointed to the prospects chatting with Raymond from human resources. "So, who looks like they'd be a good fill-in for you?"

"So far, no one has impressed me. Or Ray. See? He's got that ticking vein in his forehead again."

"Oh yeah. That's never good."

Liam leaned forward and rested his hands on his thighs. "The guy on the end is about my height and weight, so using the same costume would be easy. But he can't do a handstand for more than five seconds. And his somersaults keep going sideways."

"Well, they put out the call last night and wanted to hold tryouts today, so I guess the pickings were slim. But I don't know why the team is rushing it. We don't need a new Fin for Monday's game."

"It's Opening Day. They want Fin to do something spectacu-lar." Liam swallowed against the ball of hot resentment rising in his throat. "Those were Ray's exact words. So, if they go with one of those guys, I'll only have a day to work with him. But aiming for a spectacular stunt is going to be a stretch with that group."

He frowned as a small blonde woman he didn't recognize walked onto the field with another member of human resources. They spoke with Raymond, and then the woman shook his hand and joined the other prospects.

Slade nudged Liam's shoulder. "A late arrival?"

"I guess." He leaned forward again. The blonde pushed her sunglasses off her heart-shaped face and Liam's heart stuttered in his chest. Eyes the same blue as the sky sparkled with her smile. Her glasses rested in honey-toned hair that curved at her chin, accenting a delicate neck and shoulders. A red T-shirt with a gymnastics school logo skimmed her torso, hinting at her gentle curves and athletic build, and black shorts showed off tanned, toned legs.

She nodded at something Ray said, then tossed her glasses onto the grass. With a smile, she took a running start and then executed a few split leaps, followed by a somersault, back handspring, front handspring, and ended with a tuck jump.

"What the…" Gaze glued to the woman's face, Liam reached for his crutches. She was amazing. Not only amazing, but obviously a trained gymnast and better than him at two of the moves. Ray wanted him to weigh in with his opinion. Before the blonde's arrival, he'd been dreading talking to his prospective replacements, but now… "I need to get over there."

Slade helped him get the crutches under his arms. "She's really good. As good as you. Maybe even better than you."

Liam slowly pulled himself to standing. "You're supposed to be making me feel better here."

"Right. Um, well, you're a lot taller. And a decent roommate."

"You're no help at all." Liam clocked Slade's shin with the rubber foot of his crutch. "But you have a point on my being bigger. She's way too small to fit into my costume."

"Do you think Raymond would take the clumsy guy who can't tumble his way down the first base line just because he matches you size-wise?" Slade stopped Liam's movement with a hand to his shoulder. "You're *not* going to suggest that, are you?"

The thought ran through his mind for a second before his gut twisted at the idea. "I want to save my job but I'm not going to sabotage the team. Ray might be thinking it's the easier option because they can use the same costume but it's not the right one. But damn… she's really good. So good, there's no way Ray wouldn't choose her. So good, she might…" He glanced at his ankle, throbbing despite the painkiller he'd downed at breakfast. He needed to heal—fast —before it was too late. Maybe he could start weekly sessions in the oxygen chamber. Or…

"Li, hold up. They're heading our way." Slade's strong tone and hand squeezing his shoulder pulled Liam from his spiraling thoughts.

He shifted a step forward, careful of the crutches on the soft surface, and pasted a smile on his face.

Everything was changing. He couldn't control it, wasn't happy about it, and didn't see any way where it ended well.

CHAPTER TWO

CLAIRE

Claire caught her breath and rejoined the group, glancing at the men and women around her, sizing up the competition. She sought out Raymond and didn't know what to make of his raised brows. Was she a lot better than the others… or a lot worse? She hadn't performed in a while but the jumps and moves were second nature. Maybe she should've added a few more. Did she even have a shot? Stretching to her full height, she smiled big enough to show confidence and breathed in the sweet scent of fresh-cut grass.

When she'd dropped off her youngest sister for gymnastics practice that morning, she hadn't expected to spend her afternoon at the Riptide's ballpark. The email from her old coach alerting her to the audition couldn't have come at a better time. And the job promised to be a lot more fun than the thankless sales position at the auto insurance company. Provided she got it.

Raymond typed something into his tablet. "Thank you, Ms. Devereux. If you'll please come with me. The rest of you, thank you for coming in. Please follow the security guard to the exit." He turned without waiting for a response.

Claire blinked at his back. She wouldn't allow herself to believe she was in. This was probably the first hurdle.

She snatched her sunglasses from the grass and followed him toward the two men in front of the dugout. Dressed in jeans and T-shirts, the taller of the two was easily recognizable even out of uniform. Slade MacInnes had graced the cover of every sports magazine last season. But the man by his side, leaning heavily on crutches and sporting a smile that didn't reach his eyes, captured her attention. Dark brown hair tousled by the wind begged for her hands to smooth it. And his eyes, as rich and deep as her favorite triple-chocolate brownies, burned with an intensity that was almost magnetic, daring to draw her in and hold her forever. The nerves zinging her stomach shifted into high alert, buzzing through her blood as she continued to hold his gaze.

Raymond gestured to the man. "Claire, I'd like you to meet Liam York. He's the resident mascot and will be your go-to person. You'll be working with him closely. And Liam, Claire here was clearly the best of the try-outs, as I'm sure you agree. She graduated from Anaheim State a few years ago and was their original Anaheim Annie."

Liam's brows rose, then he smiled and his eyes danced with laughter. "No way. I didn't recognize you without the fifty-gallon cowboy hat and pair of six-shooters. Annie was a genius idea. One of the best college mascots I've seen."

She grinned. "I loved that costume. And the job, playing Annie for three semesters was so much fun. I was pretty bummed when I had to turn in the cowboy boots." She hadn't had a choice, she'd been needed at home.

Liam adjusted his crutch and extended his right hand. "It's nice to meet you."

"You, too. I get a kick out of Fin's antics. You're really good." She slid her palm against his and then his fingers wrapped around hers, warm and strong and firm. Her pulse ticked faster and awareness skittered through her like a gentle brush of a butterfly's wings. His grip tightened a fraction before releasing his hold. Her first impression had been right —he radiated heat and intensity. She tilted her head back to hold his gaze. He towered over her five-foot frame by at least a foot. A black T-shirt stretched tight across defined shoulders and strong muscles attained only through hard and frequent work. Work that wouldn't be quite so frequent now—thanks to the broken ankle. "I'm sorry about your injury."

"Thanks. I'm going to miss playing Fin. But I hope he'll be in good hands. Or maybe I should say fins." He cracked a smile and she laughed.

Smiling and shaking his head, Slade nudged Liam's shoulder. "So, Claire. I'm Slade. Where did you learn those moves? You looked like an Olympic gymnast out there."

Claire dragged her focus to Slade. What was the first baseman doing at a mascot audition? She shook his hand. "I was in gymnastics from the time I was six until I graduated from high school. Then I worked part-time as a coach at my gym through college."

Raymond nodded and added more notes to his tablet. "I know you have experience performing in front of a crowd, but our games frequently sell out. It'll be more than you experienced at your college football games."

"Our team was terrible and we weren't in a good division, so I didn't feel a lot of pressure out there. But I have competed in large gymnastics competitions where I had a lot of pressure to keep myself together and execute a detailed routine. I won't choke in front of the Riptide fans."

"Still. You've been away from performing for, what, six years?" Raymond waited while she nodded. "Being our mascot is a big responsibility. Liam will teach you everything you need to know. During games, you'll have a head set. He'll be there to talk you through it if you need help. I know it's a lot to ask you to jump right into the job, but I feel with your resume, you'll be the best fit."

"I won't let you down." She didn't fail at things. Ever. Except romance. "Does that mean I officially have the job?"

"Yes. Welcome to the team."

She wanted to cheer and turn cartwheels across the field. Instead, she clasped her hands together and stayed in place. "Thank you. I'm excited to get started."

Raymond typed in another note and then pulled his phone from his pocket. "We only have a day and a half until the home opener. If you can stick around today to fill out paper-work and work with Liam, I'd appreciate it. We don't have much time to create the shark costume. I'll call our costume designer and ask her to come in now to do your fitting. She'll need to make everything. No part of Liam's costume will fit you."

Claire glanced from Raymond to Liam. Her new co-work-er's smile was gone, replaced by stoic features.

Slade rested a hand on Liam's shoulder. "If you're making a new costume anyway, Liam could still wear his and help out."

Liam's brows shot high and the spark returned to his eyes. "I can't do the stunts, but I can still walk around and greet people here. Or drive around in the golf cart or ATV so people don't bang into me." He gestured to his cast and crutches. "And I can keep my commitments to the hospital and charity."

Raymond shook his head. "We can't have two Fins running around at the same time."

"Not two Fins. Create a new character." Slade's voice was like steel but he winked at Claire. "Can't Fin have a friend?"

She didn't think that was such a bad idea, especially knowing how much pressure she'd be under to do as good a job as Liam did. "As Fin's friend, I could shadow Liam until I have a better idea of what to do and gain more experience. It might be easier than him watching and directing me from someplace in the ballpark." Although, the idea of him watching her sent a tingle through her blood.

Liam's gaze met hers. "I promise I can play well with others."

"A new character would be a new marketing and merchandising opportunity." Raymond stuffed his phone away and began typing like mad into his tablet. "The public knows you're hurt, Liam, so we should play that up."

"No offense, Ray, but I'm not injuring myself further."

"Of course not. In the first game, Fin can come out like usual, but with his crutches. Still try to do his stunts, but falls." Pausing, Raymond lifted a brow. "Falls *carefully*, where your leg won't be compromised. And that's when the new character comes in."

"I've got it," she blurted then patted Liam on the shoulder. "If you want to keep with the shark theme, my character could be a nurse shark. And we can make her like a real nurse, wearing scrubs and a stethoscope. She can come over and reprimand Fin and point him off the field. Then the announcer can say something about how I'll be taking over while Fin recovers."

Liam nodded and a crooked smile lit his face. "Only, Fin isn't following directions. He keeps trying to sneak onto the field during games."

Laughing, she bounced up a few times on the balls of her feet, unable to check her enthusiasm. She shifted closer to him, caught up in the power of his smile and how it deepened when his gaze landed on hers. "I love it. And my character can chase him off and play up her frustration to the crowd. It'll be great."

Raymond nodded, typing faster. "We can do recorded scenes with you two in costume, too. Videos one or two minutes long, showing the nurse shark taking care of Fin, with him doing antics and being a bad patient."

"How will the scenes work if we can't talk while in costume?" Claire turned toward Raymond. She hadn't had that limitation in her college mascot days.

"There'll be music and you'll be able to convey enough with your actions. We'll add in a narrator or subtitles if necessary." Raymond punched a button hard then looked up, a smile curving his thin lips. "We'll film the first few on Monday. I'm thinking we'll broadcast them during the afternoon games while the other team is warming up, maybe in between the top and bottom of the fourth inning. And they'll go up on the website the following day. If this pans out the way I think it could, we'll sell more tickets." He glanced at Claire. "We usually have one afternoon game during the week and it can be tough to fill those seats. This just might do it."

Liam frowned. "How? I mean, I like the idea. I'm all for any way I can still be Fin. But I don't see how this will sell more seats than usual."

Raymond stroked his beard, eyes focused on the stands before his gaze settled on Liam and Claire. "Because it's going to become a romance."

"A what now?" Claire felt heat rush to her cheeks. She spun toward Liam. He stared at Raymond with the same surprise she felt.

"A romance. A few episodes in, Liam will pull out a bouquet of flowers for the nurse shark. After that, we can show their first date. The first kiss. Maybe even a fight, and then how Fin wins her back." He made another note. "Corporate will need to think of a name for the new character."

Her thoughts spun, taking in the news and tossing names around that would go well with Fin. "How about Fiona?"

Liam grinned and nodded, and even Raymond smiled. "Fin and Fiona. I like it."

"It's cute." Slade grinned, looking far too pleased. "The fans will eat it up. *Fin and Fiona swimming in the sea…*"

"Dude, you're messed up." Liam's laughter rang out and warmth washed over Claire's chest. He looked so happy, the full-on smile reaching his eyes, crinkling them at the corners. His gaze flicked to hers and shifted from friendliness to smoldering. "What do you say, Claire? Want to let the fans watch us reel each other in?"

She groaned at the pun but she wouldn't have any problem showing an attraction to Liam. "How many fish puns do you have?"

Slade rolled his eyes. "Too many. And don't worry, you'll hear them all. He's a born comic."

Raymond motioned toward the dugout. "I have calls to make and meetings to set up to get everyone up to speed on our newest mascot. Claire, let's get you squared away on that paperwork now, and then Liam can show you around while we wait for the costume designer to arrive."

She stepped toward Ray, then glanced back at Liam. "I'll see you soon?"

"I'll hobble my way up to Ray's office in a bit. My assistant here," he grunted when Slade's elbow connected with his stomach, "will make sure I get there. Then we'll strategize about Fin and Fiona's first meeting." He reached toward her and then dropped his hand back to his crutch. "I'm looking forward to working with you."

"Me too. I can imagine this isn't the way you wanted the

season to begin, but I promise to do all I can to help you. I think we'll make a great team." Claire waved and followed Raymond through the stadium's maze of hallways. She could provide the antics and stunts that Liam wasn't able to do. And the added story of a romance between the mascots might mean they'd keep her on for more than half the season, maybe even long after Liam healed. The amount they were willing to pay her to essentially have fun didn't hurt either, and would go a long way toward paying off her student loans.

For so long, she'd been the responsible one. She'd never really had the chance to be a kid. Becoming the new mascot might be her last and best shot at being responsible *and* having a little fun. And she intended to do whatever was necessary to keep the job as long as she could.

CHAPTER THREE
SLADE

Slade MacInnes was late. He sped through the hospital's hallways, following the directions for his meeting with the Wishes Granted Foundation's recipient, an eight-year-old boy named Mason. He hated being late, especially for a meeting like this. But L.A.'s horrible traffic hadn't cooperated during his drive.

Musical laughter drifted from the room where he was supposed to have arrived five minutes earlier. The tone, the bubbly happiness, tugged at something inside him. He knew that voice. And really wanted to kick himself for being late.

He stopped at the doorway and took in the perfection that was Savanna Soto. Dark hair cascaded to her shoulders and she tossed a wayward lock off her forehead and laughed again, focused on something Slade couldn't see. Creamy olive skin, hazel eyes, arched brows and perfect pink lips—her face always drew him in. Her blue dress hugged curves and a narrow waist rivaling those captured on canvas and immortalized by Italian masters. Not for the first time, he wished he knew how to paint.

A little kid in a wheelchair, wearing a Riptide T-shirt,

rolled into view. "Miss Savanna, do you think Slade can show me how he hits a curve ball?"

"Not indoors, sweetie." Smiling, she patted his bald head and then pushed his wheelchair closer to the large window that looked out over the courtyard. "He should be here soon."

Slade cleared his throat and stepped into the room. "Mason? I'm sorry I'm late."

The little boy's brown eyes widened. "Wow. You're really here."

Savanna crossed to him with graceful movements, her hand extended. "Mr. MacInnes, it's nice to see you again."

"None of this formal Mister stuff. Just Slade." He grinned over her shoulder at Mason and then captured her hand in his. Smooth, delicate, and soft. So soft. Her eyes warmed with her smile and he forgot to breathe. After a moment, he remembered to relax his grip, and the reason for his visit. He took a step toward Mason.

Savanna stepped back and gestured toward the boy. "Mason's been looking forward to this visit for a long time. And this is his mother Christine."

Slade shook hands with Christine, and then crouched beside the boy's wheelchair and shook his hand. "Hey, buddy. It's good to meet you."

"I used to play baseball. You know, before I got sick." The boy's grin spread wider in his sallow face. Dark and deep set eyes sparkled despite the painful effects of his treatment. "I liked playing first base best."

"That's the best position." Slade grinned and fist-bumped him. He settled into the visitor's chair by the bed, ready to stay for as long as the boy wanted him. "If your doctors give the okay, you can visit the ballpark and take batting practice with me."

"Really? That'll be great!" Mason leaned over the side of his chair. "Did you hear that, Mom and Miss Savanna?"

Savanna gently cleared her throat. "I'll mention it to your doctors and if we can arrange a visit, I'll make it happen."

Slade met her gaze and nodded. He didn't want to make a promise that Mason's health wouldn't let him keep. "So, what else do you like besides baseball?"

"Dinosaurs and race cars."

"Yeah? I just spent the morning driving a pretty fast car." He pulled up a picture of the cherry red Ferrari 458 GT on his phone and grinned over Mason's exclamation. "It can go two-hundred-two miles an hour." Pocketing the phone, he leaned in and lowered his voice to a whisper. "But don't tell my team manager Dusty. He doesn't like when I drive that fast."

"I won't tell anyone. I promise. Have you driven anything else? My favorite is a Lamborghini."

"I drove a Lamborghini Gallardo GT the last time I went to the speedway. That one can also go up to two-hundred miles an hour." He liked the speed, the thrill of zooming around the track. Liam had gone with him that time. He'd missed having his friend along for the morning's ride but the need to blow off some steam had outweighed wanting to wait until Liam's ankle had healed.

"Cool. I got some remote control Lamborghinis for my birthday. They don't go as fast as a real one though." His thin shoulders lifted in a shrug.

"That reminds me. I have something for you." Slade pulled a Riptide jersey from his bag and placed it in the boy's hands. "It has your name on the back."

"Wow." Mason traced his finger over the letters. "I'm never gonna take it off."

"And a new hat." He handed over the gray and blue cap.

The stylized R riding the crest of a wave on the hat's crown matched the hats the team wore on the field.

Mason's grin tugged on Slade's heart. "Thanks. This is the best day ever."

"No problem." He engaged Mason in discussions on the team, superheroes, favorite ways to spend summer vacations, and how he hit a curve ball. Mason reminded him of himself as a kid, spending hours and hours alone with only baseball and his imagination to occupy his time. Unlike Mason, his solitude hadn't been due to sickness, but to living with someone who never wanted him, no matter how hard he tried.

Toward the end of his visit, Mason's father arrived. Slade again extended his invitation to Mason's parents for the boy to take batting practice with the team, and then crouched beside Mason once again. "It was good meeting you, buddy."

"Thanks for my visit and my presents." Mason reached up and hugged him, surprising Slade by the strength in his hold. "Good luck tomorrow. Mom and I will be watching the game here. I hope you guys win."

"I'll try to hit a home run for you."

"A home run on Opening Day would be awesome." Excitement radiated from his small form. "I hope I can come to batting practice with you soon."

"Don't worry. We'll make it happen one way or another." He'd do whatever was necessary to fulfill that promise. Even if he had to somehow bring batting practice to Mason. After shaking hands with Mason's parents again, he turned toward Savanna. She'd been mostly quiet during the visit, allowing Mason to have Slade's full attention. Even so, he'd been conscious of her watching and liked the way she smiled the few times he'd caught her eye.

She gestured toward the hall and he followed her out of the room. The sway of her hips and the way her hair flowed from side to side distracted him. That is until she turned abruptly. Suddenly, she was so close he forgot to breathe.

"Thank you for coming. You made his day."

"He made mine." It was true. Slade pulled in a deep breath. A mix of spices and flowers filled his lungs, replacing the hospital's antiseptic scent. Her height put her eyes level with his mouth. She'd fit against him perfectly. "You'll let me know if he can come to batting practice with the team? I can get you a schedule. I'm hoping he and his family can come to a game too."

"We're actually taking a group of the kids to the game on the thirtieth, for Fin the Shark's birthday celebration. We have a suite reserved. As long as Mason's condition stays the same or improves, he'll be able to attend."

"That's great. I'll come up to the suite and see you and the kids then. And make sure Liam and some of my teammates stop by. If Mason can go, we could do a private batting practice for him and the kids that day too."

"With Liam getting hurt, I wasn't sure if they were still planning on holding the party but he left me a message today, assuring me that it was still on and he would be able to honor his commitments with the kids."

Slade grinned, thinking of Liam and Claire. They'd been at the ballpark until late into the evening, working on ideas, and his best friend seemed to be back to his usual happy self. "It's going to be an interesting season. Liam's not going to let a broken ankle hold him down."

"I'm glad. He's been so good to this program." Savanna pressed her lips into an understanding smile and back-walked a step. "I'll let you know if Mason is able to go to the game."

"Hey." Slade burst out louder than he'd expected, but he couldn't let her walk away. Not yet.

She stopped mid-turn, her delicate brows drawn together.

"You know, this is the first time we've been together without the distraction of a large crowd or a noisy function."

"Is it?" She took a tentative step toward his personal space.

"I wouldn't forget if I'd had the chance to do more than say *hello* to you."

She tucked her hair behind her ear, exposing the silver hoop on her upper ear. He wanted to trace the earring with his finger to see if it felt as delicate as it looked. And how she'd react to his touch. Her gaze held his a second longer but then dropped to his chest. "I should get back to my office."

"Or we could have coffee."

Her head snapped up. "Right now?"

"Why not? The cafeteria isn't far and their coffee isn't awful. We've known each other for what—three years? And I still don't know what you like to do when you're not being a miracle worker here."

"My title is Wish Granter, not Miracle Worker." She bumped her shoulder into his arm and tilted her head in the direction of the elevator. "Okay. I have time for one cup. But I guarantee you're going to be bored. "

"Don't worry. I'll think of something after you tell me your favorite color and your favorite drink."

Yes. He'd been intrigued by Savanna since first laying eyes on her at the fundraising gala for the foundation three years ago. Man—she'd looked hot in the simple red dress. Until today, he'd never had the chance to approach her. All his other visits with the kids had been arranged by her assistants.

As they rode to the cafeteria, she kept the conversation centered on the kids in the program but when they sat across from each other in an empty corner of the cafeteria, she grew quiet.

Slade sipped his coffee and settled back in his chair. Not too far, but relaxed. "So, tell me all about Savanna."

"Original." She blushed and shook her head. "There isn't much to tell."

"Also original. But something tells me you really are. So what's your deal?"

"I'm twenty-six. I've been involved with the Wishes Granted Foundation since I interned with them during my senior year of college. And what else was it that you'd said you wanted to know? Oh, right. My favorite color is teal. My favorite drink is champagne, and when I'm not working, I definitely don't spend my time racing cars around a speedway at two-hundred miles an hour."

He laughed and leaned forward, placing his cup on the table. "Have you ever tried it?"

"You have a reputation for being a risk taker. I've heard the other players talking about your escapades for years."

"Escapades?" He couldn't resist grinning at her; she'd asked his teammates about him. "Is that really what they say?"

She nodded and pursed her lips to fight the smile. "I'm afraid so. Last season, Dom Torres told me that you went sky diving during your day off in Arizona. Adam Hudson mentioned that the two of you walked on some clear bridge somewhere. And Liam has told me countless stories of how the two of you spend the off-season. Cliff diving, extreme skiing, and bungee jumping. Is there anything you won't do?"

Pleased she'd learned so much about him, he leaned back in his seat again. "Not really."

"But, don't you ever get scared?"

"It's more of an adrenaline rush." He drank from his cup. The coffee wasn't half-bad. He couldn't tell her that the rush temporarily filled the ache of loneliness in his soul. He never talked about that, but he'd suspected Liam, Dom, and Adam had figured it out. "No room for fear."

She pushed her cup aside and leaned forward, arms crossed on the table. Her smile had faded, replaced by an earnestness he hadn't expected. "How do you do it?"

"Do what?"

"Plan those things and then not worry about what could go wrong? Or do them in spite of what could go wrong?" The intensity in her voice and in her gaze pulled at him to fix whatever was troubling her.

He set his cup near hers and mirrored her position. "Worrying about something doesn't help. It only wastes time that you could spend doing something else."

"I'm really glad you asked me to coffee. I have a problem and you're the perfect person to ask for advice."

He could see by the look on her face, something was eating at her. And not whether he was going to ask her out. Though disappointed their coffee wasn't a flirt-fest, he was curious.

"Shoot." He nodded for her to continue.

"My brain seems to be wired for worry. It's pretty frustrating. I miss out on things because of it but can't seem to stop."

"What type of things?"

"Trips and experiences, and more everyday type of things that you'd do without a problem. That most people would do without a problem." Rolling her eyes, she sat back. "Never mind me. So, are you ready for the upcoming season?"

Slade glided his hand across the table until the tips of their fingers barely touched. He'd never seen her anything less than confident. Peeling back the layers and uncovering who she was and what made her tick was far more tempting than discussing his readiness to play baseball. "Tell me some everyday-type-of-things you're scared to do."

"This is embarrassing, but I once spent five minutes stuck on a high diving board paralyzed with fear. The lifeguard had to come and get me down."

"That's nothing to be ashamed of. I remember lots of kids being scared of the diving board at the community pool when I was growing up."

"No." She shook her head and color rose in her cheeks. "That happened last summer. I was with some friends and thought I could do it, but when I got up there, well, the board seemed a lot higher than I'd expected."

"Oh."

"Yeah. And I can swim, too. But I couldn't jump." She pulled her hand away. "Last week, one of the kids in the program wanted to be a fireman for a day so we took him to the local firehouse. Everything was fine until they let him slide down the pole. He did great, but wanted me to do it too. I couldn't. I stood there, palms sweating, heart pounding, looking at the gap between the floor and the pole in front of several brave firefighters and felt like the world's biggest baby. But worse, I let him down."

"I'm sure you didn't. Those kids love you."

"Yeah, but they're so brave in battling their diseases. I need to be braver too. Mind over matter, right? But I can't get over the mind part. In my head, I tell myself I can do an activity, but when I get to the actual doing, I can't follow through. It's like something inside me locks up and all the what-if scenarios rush through my mind and I can't move."

"I can help you." The words had popped out before he'd fully thought them through. But he wanted to help her, more than he'd wanted anything in a long time. And helping her would keep his mind off of obsessing over the results of the genetics swab test sitting on his desk and whether his biological family would actually get in touch with him.

After years of being alone, maybe it was too much to hope for.

"How?" Savanna's voice pulled him away from his thoughts.

How? He didn't have a clue. All he knew was that he wanted to spend more time with her. "We'll do some of the things you're scared to do. You let me know what you've always wanted to try and we'll do it together. Or I can come up with some ideas too."

"What if we're out doing something and I freeze up and panic?" Her shoulders narrowed and her fingers pressed into the table like her fear had already kicked in.

"I promise I won't get frustrated or leave you behind. We'll talk about why you're scared and get you through it. Despite whatever ideas my teammates seem to have, I research the safest places before I do an activity. You'll be safe with me." He lifted one of her hands and held it in both of his.

Her fingers relaxed, just enough, and her hazel gaze deepened to green. "I'd like to try. But what's in it for you?"

Three years of slow burning interest made his answer easy. "Spending time with you."

Her brows drew together and she laughed, relaxing her shoulders. "Wow, that's… I'm flattered, especially considering what I just told you."

"You told me that you want to face your fears. Pretty damn brave, if you ask me."

That earned him a smile. "You think so?"

"I do. Look, playing baseball is nothing compared to the stress the kids in the program face, but my job is demanding and I have some other things going on that leave me needing to blow off steam. That's where you come in."

"So helping me helps you?"

"If you want to put it that way." He gave into the urge to squeeze her hand and caress the soft skin on top. The warmth of her skin soaked into him like a gentle morning sunbeam. "I like you. I want to spend time with you. It doesn't have to be any more complicated than that."

"There are so many things I want to try. And you'll really hold my hand through it?"

He linked their fingers. "Starting now."

Her hand tightened around his. "Literally and figuratively, hmm? I'll take it. What should we do first?"

"When are you free?"

"I'm having dinner at my parents' tonight, and you probably need to do some things to prepare for tomorrow's game. How about next weekend?"

He mentally ran through his schedule. The Riptide played nearly every day during the season. Free time was hard to come by. "I have an afternoon game next Sunday. I can pick you up after that. We'll do something scary, and then have dinner. Do you trust me to plan it?"

"I do."

The simple words and the trust behind them were gratifying. He was content to sit there, drinking his coffee and holding her hand. Being with her gave him a shot of adrenaline, softer than the jolt he felt jumping out of a plane or racing a fast car, but just as addicting.

Savanna glanced at the slim silver watch adorning her wrist. "I'd better go. I need to close my office and say goodnight to Mason and his family before I head to my parents. If I'm late for dinner, my mom will start calling the area hospitals to see if I've been admitted."

Chuckling, Slade released his hold on her hand and pushed to standing.

"The sad part is, I'm not kidding." She picked up her cup

and led the way to the elevator. After punching in the number for her floor, she moved closer to Slade in the small space. "Good luck tomorrow. I hope you guys win."

The elevator stopped at her floor. Slade slid his fingers over her shoulder, then forced his hand to his side. "I'll see you on Sunday."

She nodded and stepped out of the car. "Good night."

When the doors closed again, he grinned at his reflection, feeling like he'd just hit a game-winning grand slam home run. He hadn't expected to spend time with sexy Savanna, let alone her admission. But he was just the man to show her how exhilarating taking a risk could be.

CHAPTER FOUR

LIAM

The excitement and anticipation of Opening Day was palpable at the stadium, even hours before the game's scheduled start. Liam zoomed through the hallways on the golf cart he occasionally used to get around the field. It saved him the turtle-like pace of going the distance on his crutches. He parked outside his office and dressing room, grabbed his crutches, and then hobbled to the door. The windowless room, with its pale gray walls, large metal desk, and comfortable orange couch, was home away from home—his place to decompress. Sharing it with Claire would be interesting.

She and Slade had helped him rearrange furniture to accommodate the wide path his crutches demanded, and the desk and chair the maintenance department had brought in for her. Like it or not, reminders of his *new normal* were every place he looked.

He grabbed a water from the mini-fridge and lobbed the closed bottle onto the couch. Not having the use of his hands to carry things because they were supporting his weight on the crutches was getting old—fast. He was sure Slade would eventually tire of helping him out at home, and didn't want to bother Claire by asking for her help here. Hopefully, he could manage getting into his costume alone.

Fin and Fiona's costumes hung side by side on the closet doors. Fin's outfitted in a Riptide uniform complete with a cloth cast to cover Liam's real cast, and Fiona's in blue medical scrubs. He had to admit they looked cute together.

And Claire herself... Wow. With her compact, sexy body and heart-stopping smile and kissable lips... His body tightened and he slammed down the gate on his desire. Fin was supposed to fall for Fiona. *He* wasn't supposed to fall for Claire.

His focus needed to be on quickening his recovery and making sure he kept his job. Nothing else.

Fans, the management, the team, and the media had big expectations for the Riptide this season, and Liam had big expectations for Fin. He couldn't deny the brilliant addition of Fiona, especially if the storyline received the level of attention Raymond was sure it would. It had the potential to bring a lot of awareness to the team and by extension, the team's charity. He'd do anything in the world to help those kids. At all of the hospital visits where he'd accompanied his father, back when Dad had played Fin, Liam had realized the kids had needed his dad just as much as he did. Rather than resenting the amount of time his dad had spent with them, he'd joined in with the cheering up. Ever since, he'd viewed them as the siblings he'd never had.

The door swung open and Claire breezed in, blonde hair blowing around her face like a halo. She met his gaze and a wide smile bloomed. "I'm so excited for today. You have no idea."

"I think I have a pretty good idea," he countered, but he knew what she meant. "Any first-time jitters?"

"Not yet, but I'm sure there will be." She set her purse on

the desk behind her, then frowned at the alerts pinging from her phone. Muttering to herself, she shook her head, her thumbs flying across the keypad.

He didn't like the tiny frown line that had formed between her brows. "Anything wrong?"

Claire sighed a huge expulsion of breath. "Nothing important. Just my little sister. She can be a scatterbrain and a little dramatic."

Liam pulled his costume from the door. Her phone had pinged a lot over the last two days and each time, that same line had formed. She needed a distraction and he needed that line gone. "We should get dressed. We're supposed to meet the film crew in the training room soon."

She tossed her phone into her purse then crossed to him and ran her hand down her costume's soft material. "I can't believe this is real."

"Just wait until the first time you step onto the field." He'd never forget his first time. The crowd's energy, the sheer volume of people and noise, and all eyes on him, waiting for him to perform. "Take a second to absorb the moment. There's nothing else like it."

"Okay, now I'm a little nervous."

"The pressure is huge but you'll do fine. Remember, we'll still be connected with the head sets." He slung his costume over his shoulder and headed toward the couch, careful not to catch the edge of the rug with his crutches.

Claire beat him to the couch by five seconds and pulled the costume from him. "Here, let me help."

"I can do it." But he gratefully sank onto the cushion and set the crutches aside.

She shushed him and opened the costume's zippered back. "Is your pant leg wide enough to go over your cast?"

He reached for the garment and her fingers skated over

his. The zing from the brief touch radiated up his arm. Swallowing, he closed his hand over the gray material and leaned back. "The designer added a zipper to the calf so as long as I keep that open and roll up the leg, I'll be fine. The cloth cast will hide any exposed skin and the real cast, and will hopefully be a reminder to people that I'm injured and they shouldn't get too close."

Tugging the material over his cast and then his shorts, he kept his focus on getting into Fin's skin and not how Claire was getting under his. The other leg glided on easily and he snapped the pant stirrup over his sneaker.

In the corner of his vision, Claire slid her costume up her legs and over her arms in one easy move. She even managed the zipper without any problem. Then she turned to him.

"What do you think?"

The fins extended down her arms and attached to her gloved hands via a loop over the middle fingers. From the neck down, she was a shark with arms and legs, complete with the fin on her back. From the neck up, she was still the stunning woman who'd been on his mind for the past few days.

He grabbed his crutches and pushed to standing. "I think that when Fin sees Fiona, he isn't going to know what hit him."

She grinned and checked out her reflection in the mirror hanging on the door. "I like the blue scrubs."

"Good call there." He glanced at the costume hanging off his waist. "I probably should lay back down and try to shimmy into the rest. Balancing on one leg is hard if I have to let go of one of the crutches to pull on the costume."

She shook her head and crossed to him. "I'll help."

Liam stiffened his muscles when she held the one crutch and helped him tug the costume over his arm. Having her so close messed with his senses. She switched sides and when pulling up the other sleeve, her fingers brushed along the bare skin of his forearm and bicep before running over his T-shirt covered shoulder. He sucked in a breath as his body reacted to her touch.

Not the time. Not the place. Not now. Not her.

Repeating the commands helped him get a handle on his control. Until she stepped behind him. Her hand brushed his neck where she held the material in place as she zippered the costume closed. God, if she helped him like this before every game, he didn't know if he'd make it through the first week without bursting out of his skin. "Thanks."

She stepped in front of him, cheeks flushed, and helped him loop the fins over his gloves. "Do we put the heads on now?"

"Yeah. The team doesn't ever want Fin or Fiona running around unmasked." He shifted his weight and reached behind him for the mask that hung like a hood. He couldn't have her helping again and touching his face. He'd do something to reveal his desire for sure.

Claire pulled her mask into place. The costume designer had done a great job. Exaggerated blue eyes framed by thick lashes and a friendly expression made Fiona the perfect counterpart to Fin. Claire's expression was hidden behind the dark screen but he thought she was smiling.

"I've watched Fin for years, but I'd never really thought about the person inside the costume. I guess that's true for most people when it comes to the mascots."

"I actually like it that way. When I go out, no one recognizes me. Slade, Dom, and Adam get recognized all the time. It's hard for them to live a normal life. I get a taste of it when we go places together and I really like being the anonymous friend."

"When I think of players and mascots, I don't think of them hanging out together. It's nice you can do that and they aren't some macho athletes who look down on the mascot as some kind of clown."

"I don't know how it is in every ball club or how even half of the guys in the Riptide's clubhouse feel, but those three are my best friends. Dom and I became friends a few seasons ago because one of the terminally ill kids in the charity wanted to meet us both. We spent a lot of time with him that season before losing him to cancer right before the season ended. That experience bonded Dom and me, and through him, I got to know Adam and Slade. Adam's our voice of reason, always looking out for us. And Slade, well, he and I clicked instantly. He's the brother I never had. They're all the brothers I never had."

Claire backed up to give him room as he made his way to the door. "You're an only child?"

He nodded and reached for his keys. "You? No, wait, you have a sister."

"I have five sisters. I'm the eldest. And sometimes I wish I were an only." She pulled the door closed at her back. "Are we taking the golf cart to the training room? Can I drive?"

"Sure. Thanks." He could still manage to drive but didn't want to start off on the wrong foot with her, so he tossed her the keys, climbed into the passenger side, and then set the crutches behind him. "You know, the costumes didn't always have gloves. For years, they were a solid piece where the fins covered the hands completely. But when I started, I lobbied hard for the gloves because I needed more control over the stunts. Plus, I didn't need someone to drive me around the stadium, and it would be easier to throw balls and shirts to the fans. I never even thought about how I'd need my hands free to deal with crutches. Added bonus, I guess."

The ride through the hallways and down the elevator took only a few minutes, but having Claire so close, with her arm brushing his, was enough to scramble his concentration.

The film crew set up the first shot in the hallway and had Fiona march ahead of Fin and dramatically point to the training room. Fin maneuvered into the space and looked at Fiona, waiting for further instruction. She patted the small couch along the wall and motioned for him to sit. He complied with his leg extended over the rest of the cushions. She slid a pillow under his ankle, then shook her fin at him. He hung his head and did his best to appear chastised.

Fiona nodded and turned away, busying herself with some of the equipment on the opposite side of the room. Fin picked up his crutches and kept twisting toward her, checking to see if she noticed him moving. Then he stood and hobbled into the hall. He hopped to the golf cart and started it up, continuing to glance over his shoulder. The cameraman backed up to capture both Fin's escape and Fiona exaggerated surprise as she watched him drive away and then ran after him.

Laughing hard, Liam reversed his movement and came to a stop by her side. "Nice job in there. I think our first video was a success. That one will play in well with Fin sneaking on the field."

"True." She climbed into the cart for the short ride back to the training room. "Fiona needs to pull out some tricks to keep Fin where she wants him."

He nudged her shoulder. "And where do you want me?"

"I… I mean Fiona probably wants to chain Fin to the training table."

The scene unfolded in his mind—only the table became a bed where he and Claire wrestled for control. "I would fight the chains. Unless you stayed with me."

Her breath hitched and then she cleared her throat. "You mean Fiona. Fin would fight unless Fiona stayed with him."

"Right." He eased back and climbed off the cart, remembering at the last second to grab his crutches. The last thing he needed would be to take another tumble. He blamed the blood flowing south for his momentary lapse in judgment.

The next scene called for Fin to sit on the trainer's table, leg extended. Claire stood by his side while the crew readied themselves. "I don't want to hurt you. It is really okay if I touch your leg?"

"As long as you don't smash a mallet over it, I think it'll be okay."

She rested her covered hand on his shin, light enough to barely register, but he could easily imagine the touch without the layers of fabric separating their skin. "You joke around a lot."

He shrugged. "Not always. But it's hard to be serious when we're both wearing giant shark costumes."

"You have a point." She stepped back. "And I have an idea. Would you be okay with Fiona tying Fin to the table with a few exercise bands? We could have two of the players come in and distract Fiona while another helped Fin escape."

"I'm all for it. Adam can distract you while Slade and Dom help me escape. I'll need them both if I want to move fast." He loved getting his friends in on the action and with them there, he'd have more of a distraction from Claire.

They recorded a few more videos until his friends arrived dressed in uniforms amid loud footsteps and laughing banter. From his place on the table, Liam instructed someone to lock the door so he and Claire could remove their masks for a moment, and then made the introductions, first pointing to his oldest friend. "This is Dom Torres, center fielder. Next to him is Adam Hudson, today's starting pitcher. And you know Slade."

Slade waved at Claire as she slipped her mask in place and then surveyed them with a wide grin. "You two look adorable."

Liam threw a towel at him and missed by a mile. "Shut up. But yeah, that's the idea."

Dom came to the center of the room. "Where do you need us?"

Claire pointed with her soft fins, looking far too charming in her costume for her own good. "Adam comes in first with an injury and while I'm checking him, you and Slade sneak in and untie Fin and carry him out."

Adam's laughter rang through the room. "That's great. Maybe the cameras can follow the guys and they carry him into the clubhouse."

"Easy for you to suggest when you're not the one carrying him." Slade lobbed the towel at Liam. "I like it."

Dom dramatically wobbled his knees and staggered forward. "We'll try not to drop you."

Liam shook his head and fixed his mask in place. He was surrounded by comedians. "Maybe we should stick with the golf cart. Let's get started."

The guys left and Liam adjusted his position on the table. Once the camera was rolling, Claire again came to his side and shook her fin at him. Liam lifted his arms into a shrug with fins upturned. Then she held up the exercise bands she'd tied together. The sound engineer would add in suspenseful music during editing. Liam forcefully shook his head in exaggerated movements, with the camera closing in on his face to give Claire time to slip the band over his torso and grab the other end from the floor.

The camera backed away, panning out as Fiona tied the

ends, and then Liam did his best impression of a flailing fish flopping around a boat.

Adam walked in, holding his side and grimacing in pain. Fiona rushed to his side and led him to the table on the other side of the room.

Dom and Slade poked their heads into the room, glancing from side to side like they were in a really bad suspense movie. They crept into the room, hamming up their expressions for the camera, and worked fast to free Fin.

Dom grunted as they lifted Liam from the table. "What the hell do you sharks eat?"

"Shh. No talking." Liam elbowed him and then wrapped his arms around their shoulders. As soon as they'd cleared the room and were moving down the hall, he allowed himself to laugh. "Adam's a genius. But we didn't plan this part, so I hope Dusty doesn't get pissed that I'm in the clubhouse again."

"Dusty can go to hell." Dom's love for the grouchy team manager was non-existent. "Most of the team should be warming up on the field about now. We need to head out there after dropping you off."

"Yeah, but we'd better circle back and grab Adam. Dusty made a big deal about all of us being out there to show our team commitment. I don't want him getting chewed out for being a minute late." Slade nodded to the employee who saw them coming and opened the door to the thankfully empty locker room. They set Liam down on the bench in front of Slade's locker.

"Go on. I don't want Dusty benching you guys to prove a point. Thanks for helping out." Liam waved them away and as the cameraman came closer, he picked up a sports magazine that someone had left on the bench and began leafing through it.

The door banged open and Fiona stood in the threshold, arms crossed and tapping her foot. Liam tossed the magazine aside and looked around for his crutches. But they were back in the training room. Fin was trapped. This would make for a great video. He hung his head and then looked at Fiona and shrugged with his fins upturned again.

Shaking her head, she reached for something outside the room, then brought his crutches into view.

Liam grinned. Hopping back to the training room on one foot wasn't something he'd wanted to do. Fiona handed over his crutches. Liam stood, then made sure the camera was close. He leaned down and kissed Fiona's cheek. Or as close to a kiss as he could manage, touching Fin's open mouth rimmed with rows of teeth to the side of Fiona's face. It was the best he could do.

Fiona pointed to the door, and then again in the hall, she pointed toward the training room. Fin nodded and moved in that direction. He paused at a light touch on his back and glanced to his side. Fiona's fin rested there as they walked. She had good instincts. The camera following behind them caught every moment.

When they reached the training room, he relaxed against the table. The cameraman gave him a thumbs-up and ended the recording, then left the room.

Claire hopped up on the table in one graceful move. "Was that kiss on the cheek the start of Fin and Fiona's romance?"

"I think so." It hadn't been scripted that way, but had felt right in the moment. "That okay with you?"

"Fiona is ready for whatever Fin does next." She was close enough for him to see her eyes through the mesh opening. As blue as the sky and reflecting the same *want* coursing through his blood.

Maybe Fiona was ready for Fin, but Liam sure as hell wasn't ready for Claire.

CHAPTER FIVE
CLAIRE

Claire stood in the ballpark's tunnel, seconds away from her grand entry. Her heart beat hard as nerves needled her stomach. The size of the crowd easily quadrupled the number that had attended her college football games. And the national broadcast meant that potentially millions of people would witness her debut. Amazing and scary as hell.

Deep breathing before her gymnastics competitions had always helped. So had visualizing her routine. She did the same now. Blocking out Liam in the golf cart, the chatting security and staff surrounding them, and the noise of the crowd, she ran through everything from start to finish. She could do this.

Liam's hand touched her forearm. "You'll do great. The crowd is going to love you. And I'll be right there with you. We can talk via the headsets."

"I'm ready. Let's do it."

He started the engine. "Don't forget to take a moment when you get out there. Soak it up. There's nothing like stepping onto the field for the first time."

Music poured from the stadium speakers. Liam nodded. "That's my cue."

And he was off, zooming in a lap around the field. Cheers from the crowd rose to deafening levels. They obviously loved Fin.

"It feels good to be back." Liam's voice rasped in her ear. She kept her gaze trained on the giant screen over left field which gave the crowd a close-up view of Fin's antics.

He hopped out of the golf cart at home plate and waved one crutch in the air. The camera zoomed in on the white cast covering Fin's left ankle. The crowd's collective *aww* made Claire smile. They really cared about him.

Fin made his way a few feet up the third base line and stopped at the warning track. Crutches in place and standing on one foot, Fin wiggled his body in a shark's version of The Twist. He pointed his crutch toward the crowd in front of him and the little kids in the stands copied his dance. Then he pointed the crutch out to the left side and did the dance moves again. After lowering the left crutch, he lifted the right one and danced again.

Liam's voice crackled once again in Claire's ear. "I'm almost ready for Fiona to join the party."

He lifted both crutches into the air and waved them around, getting the crowd to respond with a roar. Then he froze.

The music stopped.

He looked down at his feet, as though he was just real-izing that he was on one foot and rapidly losing his balance. The crutches flapped in the air in a frantic attempt for him to regain it. He fell backward, the crutches flew out of his hands, and he landed on his back in the grass. Claire's breath caught. Half the crowd gasped. The other half laughed as Fin wiggled from side to side in exaggerated and silly attempts to get back to standing. He failed every time.

A siren sounded and an ambulance graphic lit up the giant screen. The lights around the stadium flashed red and white.

Claire took a deep breath. Her moment had arrived.

She ran onto the field.

The PA announcer's voice rang out around her. "And here we have Fiona the Nurse Shark. She doesn't look too happy with Fin's dancing antics."

The crowd cheered. Claire blinked at the wave of sounds, slowing for a moment to do as Liam had suggested, taking it all in. Clear sky, thick carpet of grass under her feet, thirty thousand fans in the stands, the players on the field, and the cameramen capturing her every move. Never in her dreams had she imagined having an experience like this.

The sirens switched to a pulsing instrumental with a heavy drum beat. She launched into a series of handsprings and somersaults straight across the outfield. Cheers grew louder and everywhere she looked, fans were applauding. She jogged down the third base line, waving at them with both hands.

Reaching Fin, she shook her fin at him, then gathered the crutches and helped him stand. With a dramatic sweep of her arm, she pointed at the golf cart, then used her other fin to motion him over to it.

Fin hung his head, but hobbled over and climbed inside the passenger seat. Claire waved to the crowd again, then joined him.

"Fiona will be here at the park, making sure Fin follows his recovery. Let's all give her a big welcome." The PA announcement was followed by an increased cheer.

Liam twisted toward her. "Nice moves out there."

"Thanks." Excitement and happiness filled her to bursting. She drove carefully off the field amid the roar of the crowd.

"Head back to our office. We don't have to be back on the field for another few innings."

She navigated the hallways at a slow speed. Everyone they passed gave them high-fives or asked to pose for a picture.

Fifteen minutes after her on-field debut, they reached the quiet privacy of the office.

Liam locked the door behind them, then pulled off his mask. With the flick of a remote, the Riptide game lit up the small TV on the wall. He grabbed two bottles of water from the fridge and lobbed one in her direction. Leaning on his crutches, he twisted the top off and lifted the open bottle in toast. "Here's to an awesome debut. To put it in baseball terms, you knocked it out of the park."

Claire's smile couldn't get any wider. She removed her mask and raised her water. "Thanks. And here's to us being a successful team."

"I'll drink to that." His throat worked as he downed the contents of the bottle. Her gaze fixed on his tanned neck and the drop of water that ran down and disappeared beneath his costume.

Heat overwhelmed her. He really was an attractive man. Reminding herself that she was twenty-six and not some hormone-ruled teenager, she drank her water and focused on their schedule for the rest of the game. "We're supposed to be at the kids' zone in the third inning, then the fan shop in the fifth. Then we're back on the field during the seventh inning stretch where I'll challenge some little kids to a cartwheel competition. Winner gets a Fin the Shark baseball cap."

"Be prepared for lots of kids petting your costume and asking if it's really a costume or if we're real sharks." He laughed and grabbed another water. "I love that one. The adult fans are great but the kids are the best part. You'll see. They get so excited."

"I didn't realize exactly how much Fin is loved until I was down there in the middle of everything." Countless photos of Fin with little kids covered an entire wall. Confidence drooping, she paced the room. What if the youngest fans didn't end up liking her? "I know I did pretty well today, but I'm worried a lot of those kids are going to resent Fiona for sending Fin off the field. Having you out there will help them accept me."

"Hey," Liam's hand on her shoulder halted her movement. "Introducing a new character is tough, but you've done it before and you're talented as hell. Not only with the moves; your sense of timing is perfect. Besides, who can resist a cute shark like you? Fin's going to be spewing hearts out of his gills over Fiona. The kids will see that and fall for her too."

They shared a smile and Claire stilled as Liam's gaze roamed over her face. Sweat glistened on his skin and darkened his hair. She battled back the strong urge to sweep the damp strands off his forehead. Three days wasn't much time to learn about someone but she liked what she'd discovered so far. He watched her like he was interested, like he was memorizing every inch and wanted to learn more.

She shifted a step closer, enjoying the weight of the hand still resting on her shoulder, and his fingers lifted to brush through the ends of her hair. She'd never dated a co-worker. Never dated much, period. Past dates and boyfriends hadn't liked taking a backseat to the responsibilities to her family. Those responsibilities weren't quite as demanding anymore. She deserved to have some fun and her interactions with Liam proved he'd be a lot of fun.

But as much as she wanted to raise onto her toes and see how firm his lips would feel against hers, she couldn't risk anything that could potentially blow up in her face and cost her the job. She tucked her hair behind her ear and dragged her gaze away. "So, um. We should…"

Liam's hand fell to his side. He'd probably reached the same conclusion. "We should head over to the kids' zone."

"Right." She backed up a few steps and he used his crutches to put another few feet between them.

Where the chemistry between them on the field and in the office had energized her, their almost kiss initiated an awkward tension that felt as heavy as the humidity weighing down the air. Sipping the rest of her water, Claire did her best to look anywhere but at Liam.

When they finished, he tugged his mask in place and waited for her to do the same. Then he tossed her the keys to the golf cart. "You drive. I'll navigate."

Claire nodded and slid into the driver's seat. She'd done without a lot of things over the years. Ignoring her attraction to Liam wouldn't be that hard, would it?

CHAPTER SIX

SAVANNA

For the third time in an hour, Savanna checked her appearance in the full-length mirror by her closet. Slade had been mysterious on the phone. *Dress casually and don't wear high heels* had been his only clues. Not knowing their destination bugged her like crazy, but he'd had a point: if she didn't know what to worry about, then she wouldn't waste time worrying.

Instead, she'd spent the week thinking of him and trying to guess what he might have planned.

Hopefully, the dark jeans, white shirt, shrunken red leather jacket, and brown leather ankle boots would be appropriate.

She didn't think he'd suggest they go skydiving or anything that extreme, but who knew? An adrenaline-junkie might not see that as extreme.

The loud rumble of an engine burst over the late afternoon stillness. Rather than fading away, it cut abruptly in front of her apartment. She lifted the curtain away from her bedroom window. In the parking space directly across from the small patch of lawn separating her building from the parking lot, Slade swung off of a large motorcycle. A black leather jacket molded to his shoulders and torso and faded jeans encased long legs. With his boots and dark Aviator glasses, he looked sexy and a hint dangerous.

Her pulse pounded, lit with nerves and anticipation. She dragged her gaze back to his bike. Black and chrome, it gleamed in the sun. A far cry from her safety-first gray sedan parked in the next spot. Maybe she should offer to drive.

Unless that *was* the date. Her clinging to him while he sped the bike along the roads with nothing more than their clothes as protection from possible collisions.

Swinging a black helmet, Slade strolled toward her sliding glass door. A moment later, the intercom buzzer sounded and Savanna rushed to answer it. He smiled and waved through the glass and then pulled off his glasses and tucked them into his shirt collar.

She tugged the door until it slid wide enough to gain him entrance. "Hey."

His gaze roamed from her eyes to her boots and his smile widened. "You look great."

"What I'm wearing is okay for what you have planned?"

"It's perfect."

"Good." She self-consciously tugged at her jacket. "Then what do you have planned?"

"Do you really want to know now or should I keep quiet until we get there?"

Her flat shoes put her eyes level with his neck. She raised her gaze until it connected with his laser blue stare. "You mean the exciting date isn't riding on the motorcycle? I heard you pull up."

"No, but I thought we'd take my bike to get there."

"I've never ridden on one."

He stepped closer until only a foot separated them. The

scent of leather mixed with cologne beckoned her closer. "Do you want to? I promise I won't go too fast. It's a great ride. There's nothing like it."

When he put it that way, with the promise in his voice and the heat in his gaze, how could she say no? But fear wiggled its way through. "What about a helmet? I won't ride without one and I won't take yours."

"I have that covered." His fingers linked with hers and he pulled her through the open door and over to his bike. He opened a side compartment and pulled out a helmet painted in teal with tiny particles that sparkled in the sun. "This one is yours."

The bright color made her smile. "Teal is my favorite color."

"I know. You told me when we were in the cafeteria." He pressed the helmet into her hands. "I picked this up for you yesterday."

"You bought me a helmet?"

"I want this to be fun for you. I thought if you liked it enough, maybe you'd go for a ride with me again sometime."

"Slade." Her nerves quieted. "Thank you."

A shrug accompanied his grin. "We should get going so we don't miss our reservation."

"We're going to dinner?"

"Dinner will be included." He walked back with her and waited while she grabbed her purse and locked her door. "We're actually doing something that I've never done before."

She pulled up short. "Wait. What?"

"But it's safe. I swear. I did my research." He drew her helmet over her head and fastened it before donning his own. "I can't wait to share it with you."

The excitement glinting in his eyes was a contrast to the apprehension tensing her muscles and slowing her steps to the motorcycle. When he swung his leg over the bike with practiced ease and tapped the seat behind him, fresh frustration washed through her. She didn't want to be afraid anymore. She needed to break whatever it was inside her that so strongly resisted taking chances.

She climbed on behind him. "I'm ready."

"Hold on tight." He moved her hands from the sides of his waist to fully wrap around his hard torso.

Pressed against his back, she inhaled the scent of leather and Slade. The warmth of his jacket seeped through her shirt and when the engine roared to life, her pulse leapt and goosebumps dotted her skin. His hand closed over hers and squeezed, and then they were moving. Out of the parking lot, away from her home, and into the unknown.

Deathly fear rolled through her as the streets rushed by. Several minutes passed before her heart slowed its pounding. The grip she had on Slade's waist didn't ease until they slowed and came to a stop by a large gray building.

"We're here. So, what did you think of your first motorcycle ride?"

Savanna eased her hands away and climbed off the bike. "I actually liked it. Where are we?"

Slade pulled off his helmet, then unfastened hers, and locked them both to the bike. "We're taking a sunset ride in a hot air balloon."

"Wow. Of all the scenarios I pictured, that one didn't come up."

"Don't tell me that you've done this before."

"Never."

He slid his hand against hers. "First step is meeting the pilot and crew. Come on."

Slade introduced her to the guys she was about to entrust with her life, then they drove to the launch site. While they drove, Derek the pilot spoke about his several years of experience in piloting the balloons. When they reached the site, he explained how the basket and balloon envelope were laid out so that the wind aided the inflation process. Then he had Savanna and Slade help hold the envelope open while the inflation fan forced air into the balloon.

Savanna's trepidation surged when Derek lit the burner and fire blew into the envelope, but watching the colorful balloon come upright was a very cool experience. She shared a smile with Slade and allowed him to help her into the basket. She was tall, but climbing inside wasn't her most graceful moment.

Derek nodded at them. "Ready to take off?"

Her palms grew damp and she gripped the basket. "Sure."

Slade's arm slid around her shoulders. "Let's do it."

Her stomach rolled as the basket moved and rose into the air. She breathed in deep, concentrating on the feel of the wicker against her palms, and the strength of his arm around her shoulders, and not on how the trees, buildings and cars grew smaller and smaller. Derek had said the balloons could go as high as several thousand feet, but that he'd keep it to fifteen-hundred for them. He'd probably taken one look at her and seen the nerves spiking and worries spinning.

"Hey." Slade's murmur tickled her ear. "You okay?"

"Honestly, I keep thinking about errant wind gusts coming along and carrying us far out to sea. I know it's silly and he explained how the basket can't tip over, but still." She lifted her shoulders as heat burned into her cheeks. "Irrational fears strike again."

Slade cupped his other hand against her cheek. "Maybe this will take your mind off of them."

He turned her until their bodies faced each other and she released her grip on the basket. The arm around her shoulders pulled her in closer. Slade inclined his head and brushed his thumb over her cheek. Her breath caught and her lips parted, ready to welcome his. She watched his eyes and the way they seemed to darken as he drew closer. Her heart pounded all over again, but in anticipation, not fear. In need and desire.

Warm, firm lips closed over hers and his fingers continued their gentle caress. Savanna clutched his jacket, both to keep him close and as an anchor. Slade made a small sound of approval and slanted his mouth, taking the kiss deeper. A thread wove between them, binding them together. Whatever this was, it was huge, overpowering, and as heady a sensation as the most dizzying buzz she'd ever experienced.

Slade lifted his head and trailed his finger over her lips. He looked a little dazed. "So, yeah. I know my favorite part of this experience."

Smiling, she leaned into his embrace and relaxed, enjoying the peaceful glide along the air against a backdrop of reds and golds streaking across the sky.

They pointed out landmarks to each other and laughed over Derek's stories. Too soon, he said, "We're coming up on our landing. The wind is picking up, so we might have a bumpy one. I want you to crouch down, turn sideways from the approaching ground and bend your knees slightly to soften the impact. The balloon may drag and turn sideways so use the basket to lean against to ensure no injuries occur."

Injuries? Savanna tensed as the basket drew closer to the ground. She peeked at Slade. He watched the landing with the same determination she'd seen him exhibit while waiting for a pitch. Concentration, but no fear. As though he felt her gaze, he glanced up and smiled, then covered her hand with his. "No worries."

The basket bumped along the ground and came to a stop.

Derek continued to issue instructions. "Wait in the basket

for some of the hot air to be released. That way the balloon doesn't take off again when you dismount."

"Now, that would be a story." Savanna moved closer to Slade, exhilarated over the ride and relieved they'd had a safe landing. She glanced around the area outside the basket. They were in the field behind the gray building where they'd started.

"No kidding."

At Derek's okay, they climbed out of the basket and then he waved them toward a table draped in white linen. A bottle of champagne, clutches of tapered candles, and dishes of various hors d'oeuvres covered the center.

Savanna turned to Slade. "This is nice."

"This is the rest of the experience. The crew will dismantle the basket and pack up the balloon and we can take our time out here. I'm glad the wind cooperated and we were able to land here instead of another spot. My bike's in the parking lot, so there's no rush to get back anywhere." He poured a drink for them both.

She filled her plate and settled into one of the chairs. They were situated so that she and Slade would be next to each other.

He handed her a glass and then raised his in toast. "To a successful flight."

The bubbles fizzed over her tongue. Savanna set her glass aside and touched Slade's hand. Like every other part of him, it radiated heat and strength. "Thank you for tonight."

His smile bloomed, lighting his face as bright as the sun. "I'm glad you liked it. I wasn't sure what you'd think. But that *and* riding on my bike? I'm proud of you."

"So, you'd want to do this again?" Biting her lip, she waited for his response. Her earlier worries hadn't scared him off?

In a flash, he twisted his hand and linked their fingers together. "Just wait until you see what we're doing next time."

The promise, the heat in his words, and his mischievous expression were a powerful combination. He intrigued her like no one else. They were as different as could be, but somehow he understood her. Being pushed outside her comfort zone was so hard, but he didn't laugh at her fears, didn't scoff at her reactions, and didn't demand that she simply "get over it". Those things alone made him stand out. Add in the way he'd held her when they'd kissed, and the show of sweetness when he'd bought that helmet, and *whoa*...

Life wouldn't be dull with him around. It was time to break out of her safe little bubble and *live* and for once in her life, not worry over the *why's* and *how's* and simply enjoy.

CHAPTER SEVEN

SLADE

Slade smoothed his hands over the front of his button-down shirt and glanced at his jeans. He'd been on edge all day. The guys had noticed it at the ballpark and given him a wide berth. Except for Dom and Adam. They'd flanked him from the moment he'd set foot in the clubhouse, to their time in the dugout, to the after-game meal.

They, and Liam, were still with him now, as he made his way to the Pasadena coffee shop where he was due to meet his half-sister, Melanie.

The late hour ensured the shop wouldn't be full, but still, the guys wore ball caps advertising the city's football and hockey teams, pulled low over their faces. His moral support squad had insisted on tagging along and Slade hadn't fought them. He winced as a passing car's bright beams cast a spotlight on them. He loved meeting Riptide fans, but not when one of the biggest moments in his life was about to take place.

Dom clapped him on the shoulder. "You ready?"

"I guess." It was just coffee. Just a meeting. Only, it wasn't and he knew it. It was his first interaction with someone who shared his genes—well, half of them anyway. His heart beat uncomfortably and his muscles filled with frenetic energy. After so many years of wondering, hopefully, some of his questions would be answered.

Liam paused by the shop's door, leaning on his crutches. "It's going to be fine. She's probably just as nervous as you. But whatever happens, we're here."

He nodded, beyond grateful for his friends. "Thanks."

Adam's hand rested for a moment on his other shoulder. "We'll hang out but if you want us gone just say the word."

He pulled the door open and waved the guys through. The shop was empty, except for the barista behind the counter and the small, dark-haired woman standing by the counter. She turned and her brows rose.

"Slade?" She looked just like the picture she'd sent him.

"Yeah. Melanie?" Silly, he knew it was her. He walked closer.

"That's me."

He extended his hand, but she waved it aside and hugged him. Taken aback, he encircled his arms around her. And it hit him.

He was hugging his little sister. His gut churned with emotions he couldn't name.

She drew back, grinning and hands fluttering in animated gestures. "I can't believe you're here. Sit, please. Can I get you anything?"

"Ah…" He doubted he'd be able to stomach anything, but couldn't sit there without ordering.

Liam met his gaze. "Slade, we'll take care of the drinks. You go and sit down."

"Thanks." He gestured toward the guys. "These are my friends Dom, Adam, and Liam."

Melanie shook their hands and then led Slade to a large

seating area in the back of the room with two couches, some chairs, and a coffee table.

Slade took the end of one couch. "So…"

Melanie sat at the other end. She tucked her hair behind her ear. "Maybe I should start. How much about your parents do you know?"

"Not much. Only that they were fifteen or sixteen when they had me and they gave me up right away."

Melanie nodded. "Okay. That's really not much at all. We'll start with names. Mom's name is Tiffany. Your dad's name is James. They broke up after they graduated from high school but actually reconnected seven years ago and got married five years ago."

His mouth dropped open. "Really?"

"It's a sweet story. High school sweethearts who reunited through an alumni planning committee."

"I can't believe it. When I found you, I'd hoped to be able to reconnect with one parent but I didn't expect getting to reconnect with two." He glanced over as Liam settled on the other couch and Dom and Adam set drinks down and sank into the chairs. Dom reached over and patted him on the shoulder. The guys knew how bad his home life had been growing up, but he didn't need to dump that on Melanie.

"They really want to meet you, but James got called to the hospital for an emergency tonight and Mom didn't think it would be fair if she got to meet you before he did. They want to do it together. But I didn't want to postpone tonight. I've known that you've existed since I was sixteen. I had to meet you."

"What does James do?"

"He's a surgeon. Mom is a financial planner."

Mom. He couldn't think of Tiffany as Mom. Or James as

Dad. He reached for a coffee to have something to do with his hands. "So, James isn't your dad?"

A swift shake of the head was his answer. Then Melanie set her coffee aside. "My dad was bad news. I haven't seen him since I was eight, when he and Mom divorced. You also have two more half-siblings. Chloe is eighteen and Caden is sixteen."

Two more half-siblings? Whoa. "How old are you?"

"Twenty-one."

"And you all have the same dad?"

"Yep." Her lips pressed into a thin line. "But James has more than made up for him. He stepped in and has been amazing to all of us."

"I'm glad for that." Blown away by more information— hell—more family than he'd expected, Slade's heart felt like it had swelled to the point of bursting.

"Don't think that Mom and James have forgotten you. And all of us kids know about you. They talk about you all the time."

"They do?"

"Of course, they didn't name you back then, so they refer to you as *the baby*. Considering you're, what, six-foot-three? That's a pretty big baby."

"He is a big baby," Liam taunted from the neighboring table, obviously unashamed to be listening.

Laughing, she reached for her cup again. "James is built like you, long and lean with blond hair and blue eyes. Mom is on the shorter side, but still taller than me. She has hazel eyes and brown hair."

"I always wondered who I looked like, if I looked like either of them." He stroked his hand over his close-cropped hair. Savanna had said she liked the way it felt against her palms. Two days had passed since their date. He wondered what she was doing, how she would react if she'd seen him so on edge. He'd told her that he didn't experience fear.

He'd lied.

Melanie pulled out her phone. "I can show you some pictures."

"Please." He scooted closer.

The screen lit with a smiling woman. She had kind eyes, polished hair, and her arms around two kids. Melanie pointed, "That's Mom with Chloe and Caden."

Stomach tight, Slade curled his fingers into his hand to stop from reaching out and grabbing the phone. He scoured the photo. This wasn't a stranger. This was his mother. And she was hugging the kids with more affection than he'd ever experienced with Liz. Twin blades of resentment and longing stabbed his gut.

The next picture showed a tall man wearing a tattered baseball cap. "That's James when he coached Caden's baseball team last summer."

Slade's heart jerked. James had his height and build, and similar facial features. He definitely looked like his dad. Comfort softened some of the resentment.

Dom leaned forward and snagged a coffee. "I guess the apple doesn't fall far from the tree."

"Tree?" Melanie glanced between them. "What do you mean?"

"Baseball."

She twisted toward Slade. "You play baseball too?"

"First baseman for the Riptide. Actually, we all play for them."

"Wait, like the *real* major league baseball Riptide?"

Slade nodded. "Yeah."

"Holy shi—I mean, I don't follow baseball, but James does. I know he's taken Chloe and Caden to Riptide games. I think Mom may have even gone with them once or twice. This is too weird. It's like they saw you without knowing who you really are."

Slade's skin tingled. His biological parents had been in the ballpark, watching him play, and he hadn't known. Shouldn't the universe have sent him some kind of sign? Jealousy throbbed that James would've been the type of dad that Slade had always wanted—someone to come to his ball games, to discuss statistics and averages, someone who just *cared*. Maybe the love of the game had been ingrained in his genes.

Melanie tucked her phone away and stood. "The shop's going to close soon, so we should go. Mom and James are really nervous about meeting you. They're leaving tomorrow for Haiti. James is spending a few weeks working in a clinic there, while Mom volunteers at an orphanage. When they get back, we'll do another get-together. Maybe you can come to our house."

His mind whirling, Slade stood and motioned for the guys to do the same. "Sure. Sounds good. I'll see what works out with my game schedule."

"I'm so glad I got to meet you. Before I knew about you, I'd always dreamed that I had a big brother. And now I do." She blushed and then rushed on, "I mean, if you want to. I don't want to interrupt your life if you don't want that, but can I maybe text you sometimes?"

Warmth washed into his chest, easing the nerves trampling his stomach. "I'd like it if you did."

"Me too." She hugged him and then stepped back. "Thanks for coming to meet me."

"Hey, do you need a ride anywhere?" He wasn't going to leave her to walk home amid darkened streets.

"Nah. The barista is my boyfriend. He'll give me a ride home after he closes and cleans up."

"All right. But be careful." The words sounded foreign to his ears. Who was he to tell her anything?

"That's very brotherly of you." She grinned again and practically skipped up to the counter.

Dom's hand fell heavy on his shoulder. "You all right, bud?"

"I don't know yet."

Liam joined them. "That's fair. This was a lot to take in."

Adam flanked Slade's other side. "Let's go home."

Slade followed his friends out into the night. He felt both less and more unsettled than he'd anticipated. He hadn't learned why his parents had given him up, or anything about what his father's life had been like before he'd reconnected with his mother. After a lifetime of wondering, not having answers when the sources were so close was driving him crazy.

His parents were back together, and their lives seemed happy and perfect. What if he didn't fit in with them? Old feelings of worry and worthlessness, the ones he'd lived with on a daily basis from age six to eighteen surged forward and simmered under the surface.

Dom drove them back to Slade and Liam's apartment. They settled in the living room with beers and baseball highlights playing on the huge TV. Slade tipped back his bottle, draining half. "Tonight was…"

"Frustrating," Dom supplied.

"Yeah. Surreal in that I met my sister. For twenty-six years I've been wondering about my family and now I've met one member. But the rest? The thing with my birth parents getting back together, going to our games, and yeah, frustrating sums it up. I feel like I have more questions than answers." He shook his head and contemplated the contents of his bottle.

Liam sat next to him with his foot propped onto an ottoman. Dom sat in the recliner to Slade's right and Adam sat on the floor. Slade couldn't imagine going through the evening without having them there. For years, they'd been his family, there for him through injuries and hangovers and playoff celebrations and the everyday stuff that everyone took for granted. "Guys, thanks for being there."

Adam reached over and tapped his beer bottle against Slade's. "We'll be at the next one if you need it too."

Slade nodded his thanks. He was keyed up. Thoughts spinning out of control without knowing which way to go. Was this what Savanna experienced when she'd mentioned the countless scenarios that ran through her brain? If so, he understood and she was right: it sucked.

Focusing on her helped calm him. He couldn't wait to see how she'd respond to what he had planned for their next date.

But for now, he'd enjoy an hour with his makeshift family and pretend for a little while that his life wasn't as complicated and everything was as simple as drinking a beer with his boys and watching some baseball.

Savanna

Large gray plastic rock formations jutted out of the walls at different angles. Colorful holds in different sizes dotted the space from floor to the thirty-foot high ceiling. Savanna stood on the spongy rubber floor, watching as Slade scaled the entire wall in under a minute. He didn't wear a harness, didn't worry about falling. When he reached the top, he twisted and waved at her.

Her stomach tightened. "What are you doing? Don't let go!"

Beside her, one of the employees laughed. "Slade's fine. He's holding on. But coming down is always harder than going up."

He really wasn't helping her feel better. She held her breath as Slade reached for foot holds that were a stretch for his long frame, bit her lip as he missed one and slipped, saving himself by grabbing onto a hand hold at his side, and then sighed in relief when he finally touched the ground.

Nearly two weeks had passed since their time in the hot air balloon, thanks to his team's road trip and then the evening ball games at the Riptide's park. He'd mentioned not having much free time during the season and the fact that he wanted to spend his day off with her made her feel special.

She turned to Slade with her hands on her hips. "Something tells me that you've done this before."

His lips twitched and he patted the wall. "Once or twice. If you've never gone rock climbing before, a gym is a great place to start. Liam and I come here sometimes to get some practice in before we hit an outdoor climb. They have a good selection of routes."

He ran his finger over the harness at her waist. They'd already gone over how the rope attached to the harness worked to anchor her and how the rope also attached to a person on the ground. That person would secure the climber, keeping a close eye on the climber's progress and letting out slack to the line by releasing the belay, a special device that locked the rope, a little at a time as the climber slowly ascended. The person on the ground, called the belayer, would prevent her from falling to the ground if she lost her footing and slipped off the wall. Slade was qualified to be her belayer, holding her rope as she climbed, but if he did, then they couldn't climb at the same time. "You ready to give it a try?"

Her palms were sweating. "Uh, sure."

Slade laced their fingers together. "I told you I'm all about safety. This place hasn't ever had an accident. They check their equipment all the time and their employees are trained. I wouldn't bring you someplace if it wasn't safe."

"They made us sign a waiver when we arrived."

"People sign waivers all the time. There are even waivers on the back of baseball tickets."

"I know. You're right." She squared her shoulders and smiled at him, and then at the employee, Elias, who would act as her belayer.

Elias went through the safety checks and let her see how he'd secured the rope to his own harness. "We're good."

She dipped her hands into the chalk pouch and studied the colored rocks, seeking out the largest ones. The rock climbing shoes she'd rented were tight but she hadn't wanted much wiggle room. She stepped on a large red rock and gripped a yellow hold not far over her head.

"The purple one on your left would be a good foot hold." Slade's voice came from her left, but she didn't dare turn her head and thank him. Total concentration was paramount.

She reached it and then grabbed an orange hold with her hand. The rope loosened and then tightened as she climbed. Some of the holds were so small, she didn't see how anyone could use them for more than a fingertip grip.

Every step took her higher and higher off the ground. A glance down for her next foothold showed she was halfway up the thirty-foot wall. Her stomach dropped. The ground looked so far away. What if the lock holding the rope broke, or the anchor fell out of the ceiling? There would be nothing stopping her fifteen-foot drop.

Her hands shook and sweaty palms slipped in their grips.

She couldn't move.

Slade moved into her field of vision, climbing the wall with ease. "I'd go for the blue rock by your knee next. Then grab the pink one with your right hand."

"Um, I don't think I can."

"Sure, it looks hard, but if you push up onto your toes and stretch to grab the pink rock first, your left foot will be able to reach the blue hold."

But doing that could end with her slipping off and swinging in mid-air. And she was trusting her safety to someone else. And if the equipment broke, fifteen feet down was a long way to fall, even with the safety mats on the floor. Her heartbeat raced and a wave of dizziness swept over her. "Slade, I can't move."

He switched his hand grips and footing until he rested on the rocks closest to her. "Tell me what's wrong."

"When I told you earlier that I'm not too good with heights, I should have been more honest. I'm terrified. This is scarier than I thought it would be." She swallowed hard, not wanting to disappoint him or herself. "My arms and legs are shaking. I really don't know if I can keep going, or even move at all."

He pressed his right jaw against the wall so she could see most of his face. Sober eyes filled with understanding latched onto her gaze. "Even if you stop here, you did great for your first climb. You're more than halfway up the wall and this isn't even the easiest route. If you want to go back down now, it's fine."

"I hate failing."

"Hey, this isn't failing. Let's go down. Take a break, give your muscles a chance to rest, and if you want, try it again." He turned his head and shouted down to Elias and then smiled at her. "Just let go of the holds. Elias will do all the work of lowering you."

The thought of letting go sent an icy roll of fear through her stomach. But she couldn't stay on the wall forever. Holding her breath, she lifted her fingers off the holds one by one.

"Good job. You're doing great," Slade crooned beside her. "And you're fine. I promise. You can hold onto the rope if you want. Now, just push off the wall, or lift your feet from the holds."

Keeping her gaze locked on his, she complied while her heartbeat thundered in her ears.

For a moment, she was suspended in the air. Then, the wall started to move. The holds slowly rose higher and higher. Her stomach dropped like she was on a carnival ride, but Elias lowered her steady and smooth. She reached the ground before Slade and let Elias unhook her from the rope.

Slade joined her a minute later, hopping to the ground with athletic grace. He slipped his arm around her shoulder and kissed her temple. "You really did a good job. Do you want to try again or should we call it a day?"

The gym had grown more crowded. She watched kids climb the wall like it was the easiest thing in the world. She'd bet the kids involved with the Wishes Foundation wouldn't wimp out. All around her, people were having fun. No one was cowering in fear. Annoyance at herself, at her weakness, burned hot. Leaving with a failed attempt wasn't an option. "I want to do it again."

Grinning, he rubbed her shoulder. "All right. Just pick a route."

"Maybe I should try the easiest one."

He led her to another wall. "Follow the white tags

sticking out of the rocks. It's pretty much a straight shot up and all the holds will be the same size."

She stopped him before he could turn to find Elias. "Could you belay me this time?"

He brushed his fingers over her cheek. "Absolutely."

They went through the rope hook up and all the safety checks and then Slade bent and kissed her. "You've got this. I won't let you fall."

Savanna versus the mountain. She moved into position. The holds were larger and closer together, reminding her almost of a ladder. Her stomach still dropped when she glanced down for a foothold, but Slade on the ground, watching her, holding the rope and removing the slack as soon as she moved, restored her resolve to keep going.

The top grew closer and closer, until she'd finally grasped the last hold.

"You did it!" Slade's cheer made the accomplishment even sweeter. His grin matched her own as she surveyed the gym from her bird's eye view. "You ready to come down?"

"Please." Excitement didn't fully mask her unease at being up so high. She breathed easier as he lowered her to the ground.

He unhooked their harnesses from the rope and then hugged her. "I'm so proud of you."

"Yeah but it was only the beginner route."

"So what? You *are* a beginner."

A group of kids came over, calling Slade's name, asking to take photos with him, and for him to sign their ball caps or T-shirts. He smiled and posed and shook hands and received hugs. When the crowd dwindled, he reached for her, his fingers closing around hers in a secure clutch.

"Ready to get out of here?"

Leaving the gym on a high note worked for her. Three

more people stopped him in the parking lot. He chatted with them and took a photo, then wrapped his arm around her and bid them goodbye.

She studied his profile as he maneuvered the sleek car out of the parking lot. "That happens to you a lot, doesn't it?"

"More so now, thanks to my performance the past few seasons and the endorsement deals I have. I love meeting the fans but yeah, privacy goes out the window. I don't mind as much as some of the guys, but it can be hard to relax if you're worrying about whether someone is snapping a photo of you every second. The team doesn't want any negative publicity, and there's a code of conduct we're supposed to follow. We're judged on things both on and off the field."

"That's hard."

"It can be, but I don't worry too much. Worrying is a waste of time." He shot her a grin. "How about dinner at my place?"

"Can you cook or is that going to be another adventure?"

Laughing, he switched lanes and sped onto the freeway. "I can do basic things but tonight we're ordering from the restaurant on the first floor of the building."

He drove fast, telling her about the time that he and Liam had gone rock climbing at El Capitan in Yosemite National Park. She'd noticed that most of his stories included Liam, Dom, Adam, or all three. He never mentioned his own family. Curiosity ate at her but she wasn't sure how to bring it up in case she'd hit a sore subject.

When they entered the elevator in his building, he hit the button for the seventeenth floor. He'd neglected to mention that he lived in the penthouse.

The apartment had wide, open rooms, large windows, a huge balcony, and luxury kitchen. She peeked at the view then backed away from the window. "It's private up here."

"Liam and I like it. We picked up Dom's lease when he moved out. Our old place was like a shoe box, way too small and cramped. This is better."

"Better is an understatement. This is gorgeous, and big enough to fit your whole team."

"It has, on occasion." He shrugged. "I spent enough time being lonely while I was growing up, so yeah, I like having people around."

"Did your parents work a lot?"

"Do you want a drink?" He strode to the bar and took out a bottle of scotch and two glasses.

Savanna slowly approached him. She didn't care for scotch, but his tight movements and uneasy expression suggested she'd struck a nerve with her question. "We don't have to talk about something if you don't want to. It isn't easy for me to talk about losing my sister or how my parents handled it at the time, so I understand. I really do."

He set the bottle aside. The sympathy in his gaze caused a lump to rise in her throat. "I didn't know you'd lost your sister."

There was a hollowness in her heart, a space that swelled and ached whenever she thought of Molly. "My sister was diagnosed with a rare blood cancer when she was seven years old and I was eleven. She battled it for three stressful and sad and chaotic years. After she died, my parents were like ghosts of their former selves. I was dealing with losing my best friend and so angry that we hadn't been able to save her or to at least take her to see a Broadway show in New York like she always wanted to do. But the medical bills were piling up and she died before my parents were able to make that wish come true."

"That's why you work as a wish granter."

"I was too young then to help her before she passed. But I can help other kids and make sure they get their wishes."

"You're amazing." Slade slid his arm around her and drew her against his side.

"No. I'm not." She leaned into him, absorbing his strength, and more than ready to turn the topic of conversation back to him. "Do you have any brothers or sisters?"

"Well…" His other hand moved restlessly up and down her forearm. "I just found my half-sister. Met her for the first time last night."

"Wow." She couldn't imagine Slade never having met his own sister.

"Yeah." He sighed and returned to pouring the alcohol. "I was adopted as a baby. My adoptive mom died when I was six, and then I went to live with her aunt who was in her fifties and didn't want to raise a kid at that point, so she was pretty hands-off. Didn't care what I did as long as it didn't cause problems for her."

"I'm sorry." She longed to reach out to him but couldn't tell if a touch would be welcomed. Finally, the questions she'd been too hesitant to ask were being answered.

He turned the glass around and around, studying the contents. "Even back then, I loved baseball. All that time alone left me with plenty of hours to study the game and work on my swing."

"Still, she must be proud of your accomplishments. Does she ever come to your games?"

"She passed away when I was in my first season of minor league ball. I wouldn't say she was proud. My mom had left a lot of money, so as long as her aunt took care of me, she received a monthly allowance. I'd grown up living in her house, but didn't feel like I was actually living with her, if that makes sense."

"I'm so sorry." How awful. Her heart ached for the lonely little boy and the man who still carried around the scars.

"I survived."

Surviving wasn't the same thing as growing up in a house filled with love. As smothering as her parents had been with their rules after Molly had died, they'd been equally as giving with their time and attention.

He downed the scotch and then pulled himself another glass. "I did one of those genetic swab tests. Found my half-sister, which led to my birth parents. I haven't met them yet."

"I'm sure they're going to love you."

His lips pinched together and for a moment, his eyes filled with a lost hopelessness that pushed her to move. She curled her fingers around his, willing reassurance and comfort to flow into him. He blinked and stared at her untouched glass like he was seeing it for the first time. "You're not drinking. You don't like scotch, do you? I'm sorry."

Touching his hand wasn't enough. His kiss had distracted her in the hot air balloon. Returning the favor would be her pleasure. She slid her hand to the back of his neck and gently guided his head until his lips reached hers. They were soft and open, receptive and responsive. Savanna slanted her head and deepened the kiss, teasing her tongue along his lower lip until he spun her with a groan and pressed her back against the bar.

His hands clamped and flexed on her waist and his tongue played with hers in slow licks and lazy caresses. She clung to his shoulders, then ran her hands down his biceps and up over his neck. Muscles tensed and shifted under her hands as she pulled him closer.

The front door banged open and then closed. "Slade?"

At Liam's call, Slade eased back. "In here, Li."

Savanna brushed at her hair and took a sip of the scotch.

She coughed as it burned into her throat. Chuckling, Slade pulled the glass from her hand. "You don't have to drink it. I don't have champagne here but we can get some with dinner when we place our order."

The thump of crutches on hardwood got closer and louder. "Dinner?" Faster than she would have thought, Liam stood in the doorway. "What are we having? I vote for pizza. Savanna, they do a really good job of it downstairs."

"Pizza and champagne sounds great." She shook off her disappointment that a dinner for two had turned into a dinner for three. A chance to witness—to study—the dynamics of Slade and Liam's friendship might help her better understand him. Strong and braver-than-hell Slade had been a turn on and made her feel safe. But his vulnerable side, and her feeling that he didn't show it to many people, that side brought out her protective instincts.

Maybe their arrangement didn't have to be so one-sided. Maybe she could find a way to grant his innermost wish, too.

CHAPTER EIGHT

CLAIRE

Three hours before game time, Claire pulled her car into the driveway of her family home. The sprawling house looked the same as it always did, but ever since she'd moved out, returning home felt different. She couldn't put her finger on why. Maybe because it wasn't officially home anymore. Or maybe because she still felt guilt over the need to lay claim to her own space, and to be in a place where she didn't have to cater to anyone's demands or schedules but her own.

Not that she'd fully escaped those old demands. But things were a lot calmer now. Two months into having her own apartment and almost one month into having the best job ever had a lot to do with that.

She let herself inside and sorted through the mail littering the small table by the door. Silence greeted her. She wasn't sure who she'd find home on a Saturday afternoon. "Anyone home?"

Lauren bolted down the stairs, long hair flying behind her like a cape, and grabbed Claire in a tight hug. "You're here."

Claire's breath rushed out of her lungs and she extracted

herself from her youngest sister's squeeze. "I just saw you last week."

"Yeah, but you driving me to gymnastics isn't the same as you living here."

True. "I just stopped by to check the mail. The post office said rerouting my mail could take a while."

Lauren pouted and crossed her arms over her chest. "You're not staying for dinner?"

"I can't. I have to go to work." She picked up the junk mail and headed down the hall and through the living room.

"Do you still like your new job? Have you met all the players yet? Are they nice? Some of them are really cute." Lauren's rapid-fire questions followed Claire into the kitchen.

The very messy kitchen. Claire stopped in the middle of the room. "What the heck happened in here?"

Lauren glanced around the space. "What?"

"The overflowing dishes in the sink. The used pans on top of the oven. The crumbs all over the counter. The sections of newspaper strewn all over the floor."

"Oh." Lauren shrugged. "I guess I didn't notice."

More likely, Claire hadn't been there to nag and remind people to keep things clean. "Where are Krissy and Ginger?"

"Laying out by the pool. Hey, since you're here, can you make your famous lasagna?"

Claire shook her head and stepped over Lauren's backpack and pile of notebooks. She tossed the junk mail into the recycle bin and glanced into the yard. Her twin sisters were draped over lounge chairs, laughing with their phones in hand. "What about Amanda and Jen?"

"They're both at work and should be home by five. Please stay and have dinner with us. We haven't all spent time together in forever." Lauren's wide eyes rivaled a puppy dog's pleading stare. Her just-turned fifteen-year-old sister was very much the baby of the family and Claire had a hard time telling her *no*.

She opened the dishwasher, intending to load some of the contents of the overburdened sink, but it was jammed full of dirty dishes. Seriously? How did her sisters not notice? "Dad's at work?"

"Yep. But I saw him at breakfast. He said there were a lot of surgeries today." Lauren shrugged and picked up a glass of water from the table. "I know I've always said I wanted to be an anesthesiologist like Dad, but I don't think so now. He works *a lot*."

"Mmm hmm." Claire glanced at his work schedule listed on the calendar that held her sisters' appointments, sports, schedules, and activities. The hours he put in at the hospital had been the source of some horrible fights between their parents. Claire had just turned eleven when her mother had walked out of their lives. She remembered the harsh words and accusations and the feeling of being a burden. After Mom had left, she'd promised herself that her younger sisters wouldn't ever feel that way. She'd take care of everyone.

Krissy and Ginger came through the French doors that led to the yard. "Hi," they said in unison.

Lauren thrust a worn recipe book in Claire's direction, with the page already opened to the Italian dish. "The lasagna doesn't taste the same if you don't make it."

Krissy's brows rose. "You're making your lasagna? That's my favorite."

"Mine, too." Ginger, her carbon copy in looks and attitude, chimed in. They often joked that the seventeen-year-old twins shared the same brain. Especially when they moved and spoke in sync. Twin magic, Dad had called it, and the term had stuck.

"Guys, I really don't have time." She spied the piles of

clothes in front of the washing machine in the adjoining laundry room. "What's going on? Are you all on strike? This place is a mess."

The twins shrugged, then Krissy pointed toward the laundry. "Amanda was going to do that tomorrow."

"Okay, but what about the dishes?"

"It's Jen's week for dish duty. When you moved out, we changed up the chores, but I guess it's not working out so well."

"You think?" Claire took one look at the chore schedule she'd kept on the fridge. Apparently, they'd abandoned her system as soon as she'd left. The clock hanging over the sink showed that she could spare a little time. Enough to throw the lasagna together, anyway. "Okay, here's the deal. If you want me to make the lasagna, then two of you can get started on washing and drying the dishes, plus run the dishwasher. And the other one can help me straighten up in here and cook."

Lauren bounced on her toes. "Yay. I'm glad you're staying. I'll help you. The twins can do the dishes."

"Do me a favor and start a load of laundry too." She checked the contents of the fridge. "I'm glad someone remembered to at least buy groceries."

"We ordered from the store's website and they delivered. The only thing we had to do was put everything away." Krissy squirted soap over the dishes. "It was super easy."

Ginger wrinkled her nose at the sauce crusted on a large pot. "Maybe we should order a housekeeper again too."

Claire preheated the oven, then grabbed the only clean baking dish left in the cabinet. They hadn't had a housekeeper in years. "Considering the state of the house, I'm sure Dad would agree."

Lauren and the twins kept up a rambling conversation as Claire layered the lasagna. While it baked, she helped Lauren search for her missing "lucky" leotard she insisted she needed for an upcoming gymnastics meet.

When her other sisters came home at five o'clock, Claire gasped at how much time had passed and bolted out the door. She was due at the ballpark in twenty minutes and the drive would likely take her more than thirty.

Thanks to traffic, forty minutes passed before she entered the stadium's employee parking lot. She grabbed her purse, pulled out her badge, and jogged toward the entrance. She couldn't afford to be late yet. Maybe no one had noticed.

Yeah right.

She flashed her badge at the security guard and increased her pace. Rushing to the third-floor office, she bypassed the elevator and ran up the stairs. The team wanted the mascots to be visible to the fans on the concourse prior to the game. People would see that she wasn't there with Liam. Even if the fans didn't notice, the staff would. Raymond had been pleased with her performance so far. She couldn't let that change.

Her purse caught the edge of a maintenance cart and yanked her back. She stumbled into the wall, cursing as her shoulder met concrete.

"Claire?" Liam, dressed as Fin, slowed to a stop on his golf cart. "I tried calling your phone. Are you okay?"

Rubbing her shoulder, she pushed away from the wall. "Sorry I'm late. I'll be dressed in under a minute."

She slid past him, jogged the remaining steps to the office, and dropped her purse on the floor. Her damn shoulder throbbed. Hopefully, it wouldn't hold back her performance. No one could see her wince in pain anyway during the game. The costume made sure of that.

The golf cart stopped in front of the door. Liam hopped off, grabbed his crutches, and lumbered into the room. The door closed at his back. "Are you getting in a pre-game workout by jogging around the floors?"

Laughter huffed out at the thought. "Right. That's it."

She tugged on the costume, tripping as her sneaker caught on the material. And then the zipper got stuck on the fabric. "Damn it, damn it, damn it."

"Hey, relax. We're good."

"No, we're not good. We're due out on the concourse."

"If you need more time, Fin can always pretend he locked Fiona in a closet so he could have fun on the field."

"Raymond's not going to buy that if he's out there." She sat on the couch and worked the material free of the zipper's teeth.

He came closer and laid his hand on her shoulder. "I wouldn't throw you under the bus. I'd tell Ray that you were stuck in a traffic backup caused by an accident or road construction."

Her previous sales job had been cut-throat, with co-workers stealing customers and an everyone-out-for-them-selves environment. She had never expected that Liam would back her up here. "Well, thanks. I appreciate it."

"Just curious, but why were you late?"

"Lasagna and a missing gym leotard."

She caught his grin through the mesh of Fin's mouth. "Yeah, I hate it when that happens."

They both laughed and he nodded toward the TV. "Today's episode of Fin and Fiona is The First Kiss. We can tune in right here during the fourth inning."

"With everything that's gone on today, I'd forgotten. I'm glad Raymond was right about the fans loving the Fin and Fiona storyline." Resisting Liam had been harder than she'd thought. Just one look into those laughing brown eyes and she'd melt. He made her wish for things that she shouldn't. She stood and slid the zipper closed.

He moved backward, but his crutch landed on her purse and fell away from his grip. His body pitched to the side and he flung out his arm and casted ankle. Claire sprang forward. She couldn't have him land on either of those. Yanking the front of his costume, she twisted toward the couch. His weight and momentum took them both down and they landed in a heap of tangled limbs.

"I'm sorry, I'm sorry." Buried beneath him, she panted the apology. She *never* left her purse on the floor. "Did you bang your ankle?"

"A little." He pushed up on his arms but she couldn't see his eyes through the dark mesh of the costume. "Can you pull off my mask?"

"Sure." Berating herself, she slipped it off his head. His eyes kindled with that familiar spark and his dark hair was tousled in a sexy mess. She could picture him looking this exact way after a night spent together. Dragging her thoughts from going in that direction, she smoothed the strands, desperate to fix something after the near-disaster she'd caused.

His breath stilled when her hand tangled in his hair. And she realized she probably shouldn't be touching him like this. She lifted her hand, but he shook his head. "Don't stop. I like it."

Her blood beating a steady thrum, she returned her hand to his hair. His gaze roamed her face and then settled on her mouth. He shifted his body and tugged his hand free of their tangle. When his finger trailed from her temple to her chin, her eyes fluttered closed. The touch was like thousands of points of electricity pulsing against her skin.

She opened her eyes. Liam's gaze held hers captive and

he traced his finger over the shape of her lips. "Fighting this hasn't worked. If anything, it's made me want you more."

The words spoken in the roughened tone were both arousing and gratifying. She hadn't been the only one who'd suffered. "So maybe we should stop fighting it."

A slow, dangerous smile spread across his face. He moved his hand to her throat and stroked her skin with a feather light caress. Claire left one hand buried in his hair and slid the other to his neck, massaging the muscles.

Liam groaned and lowered his head and his mouth crashed down on hers faster and hotter than she'd expected. His lips coaxed hers apart and she let his tongue slide inside to dual with hers. He kissed a trail to her jawline then down her neck in a series of nips and licks that weakened her muscles and heated her blood. Tugging his hair, she nudged him until he returned to her mouth. His urgency matched hers and his body blanketed her, wrapping them in their desire.

A knock pounded on the door. Claire jolted and knocked her forehead into Liam's. "Damn it."

He pulled away, rubbing his forehead, and rolled to the floor. "Just a second," he called out as he reached for his crutches.

Claire sprung to her feet. She adjusted her costume, slipped her mask in place, and helped Liam put his on.

When she opened the door, Tim, one of the security guards, stood with his hand on his radio. "You guys all right? Our guest singer for the National Anthem was late, but she's ready to go now. You need to get on the field."

They were much later than she'd thought. Claire groaned and glanced at Liam. "Sorry. I had some costume trouble."

"I'll have them hold the elevator for you." Tim stepped away, speaking into his radio.

Liam locked the door and climbed into the golf cart. He rubbed Fin's fins together. "Time to burn some rubber."

She started the engine and sped down the hall. Her attraction to Liam couldn't get in the way of doing her job. "Listen, about what happened…"

"It was a good first kiss, starting with the crash and ending with a bang." He raised his hand to his head.

Laughing, she glided the cart onto the empty elevator. "Seriously. We can't let it affect things here."

He laid his hand on her thigh. "Believe me, I wouldn't do anything to jeopardize this job. On the clock, we'll make sure to keep a better watch on the time. But off the clock, all bets are off."

A shiver tore through her. Anticipation rolled together with wariness. Losing focus of her responsibilities wasn't an option. And Liam proved to be the biggest distraction she'd ever had.

CHAPTER NINE

LIAM

Fin the Shark's birthday festivities were always a big event. Liam drove the golf cart decorated with balloons and streamers through the stadium, waving and nodding at all of the well-wishers he passed. The early afternoon Sunday game had started with a visit from other mascots in the area. He'd sat in a chair while they held a dance-off on the field. Claire, as Fiona, had won. In his opinion, no one could match her moves. The crowd had agreed.

It had been followed by a photo op with a huge sheet cake and videos from all of the players wishing Fin a Happy Birthday.

All in all, a good day so far, and they were only at the top of the fifth inning. Tie score, too. Hopefully, the team could pull off a win.

Beside him, Claire held the small cake they were delivering to the kids from the Wishes Granted Foundation. "It's sweet that you wanted to be with these kids when the fans sing *Happy Birthday* to you. They're going to be so excited about being on TV."

"I want to make sure they enjoy their experience. The best suite, being on TV, and then batting practice with Slade after the game." For hours now, he'd been strictly professional. Their kiss from the previous day lingered in his mind, followed by more before they'd said goodnight and another this morning before they'd headed to the field, played like his own highlight reel. He could still feel the way her lips had softened under his and how her body had melted as they'd kissed. One taste of Claire wasn't enough; he fully intended to do it again soon.

He slowed to a stop outside one of the luxury suites. "We're here."

Claire hopped out of the cart and waited for him to grab his crutches before she opened the suite's door. A sea of small faces swung in their direction and then the kids erupted into cheers.

Happiness and satisfaction burst like the brightest fireworks. Grinning, Liam eased into the room and accepted hugs flung at him from all directions. This was why he loved his job. Making them happy was the best feeling ever.

Savanna came to his left side. "Guys, be careful of Fin's ankle, okay?"

She directed their attention to the cake Claire had set on the table. The kids swarmed her too and then one asked if she and Fin were getting married. Claire lifted her fins in a shrug before rubbing the kid's head.

One of the cameramen entered the suite with Tim from security. They gathered the kids around Fin and then directed their attention to the huge screen over left field.

As the PA announcer began to sing, "Happy Birthday to you…" the kids joined in, singing at the top of their voices. The room echoed with the sounds, with half the kids pointing at the screen and exclaiming over seeing themselves. Chaos in the best possible way.

After the cameraman and Tim left, Savanna dished out the cake and Liam and Claire distributed custom baseballs with Fin's likeness to each of the kids. Leaning against the table to keep his weight off his leg, Liam grabbed three of the leftover balls and started juggling. The kids laughed and cheered and shouted for him to throw the balls higher and higher. He complied and did all of the tricks he could with his limited mobility, then finished his routine with a flourish and a bow.

Being stuck on the sidelines sucked. Juggling wasn't the same as turning somersaults or dancing on the field. But it was better than nothing.

They stayed with the kids until they had to head to the field for the seventh inning stretch and *Take Me Out to the Ball Game*. Liam sat in the golf cart waiting while Claire led three little girls in turning cartwheels on the third base warning track. She was developing her own fan base.

For the rest of the game, they stayed on the sidelines, cheering with the crowd. The game was tight, exciting as the teams took turns owning the lead. In the bottom of the ninth, with two outs and Dom on base, Slade stepped up to the plate. He launched the ball high into left field. It sailed into the stands and gave the Riptide two runs to win the game, eight-to-six. The team crowded onto the field, piling into a massive celebration, and Claire threw her arms around Liam, squeezing him tight as the stadium vibrated with waves of cheers.

When they returned to the privacy of their office, Claire pulled off her mask and unzipped her costume. She tossed him a cold bottle from the fridge, then stood in the middle of the room, gulping down a bottle of water with her costume hanging off her waist. "I can't wait to get out of Fiona's skin. It's too hot today."

"Thanks." The water would do until he could grab a beer later. "How's the shoulder today?"

She rolled up her T-shirt sleeve and showed him the bruise. "Still tender, but I'll be back to two-handed stunts tomorrow."

He shed Fin's outfit and he downed his water as he studied Claire removing her costume. "Do you want to grab a drink somewhere? Maybe dinner?"

Her brows rose and her mouth worked open. "I—" She cast a glance to her costume hanging on its hook. "We're not on the clock."

"Nope. Not now. Not until tomorrow afternoon. So what do you say? Will you help me celebrate my birthday?"

Her head cocked to the side. "I don't think Fin's birthday celebration extends beyond today's game."

"Maybe Fin's doesn't, but mine does. Today actually is my birthday."

She shot him a disbelieving look. "Is it really?"

He grabbed his wallet and held out his license. "There you go. Proof."

"Well, happy twenty-seventh birthday." She glanced at her T-shirt and shorts. "I need a quick shower first."

He waved her on. The small bathroom attached to the office had a tiny shower stall. While she showered, he answered birthday texts from his parents and one from his cousin Hunter in New York. Hunter worked at a children's toy company and always sent him the latest must-haves for the kids he visited in the hospital. He'd need to get some special things for Mason.

Claire emerged from the bathroom in jeans and a red tank

top that showcased her toned muscles. "Where did you want to go?"

"There's a bar five minutes down the road. It's tradition to go there on my birthday, but it's kind of a dive. We can go someplace else if you want." The guys would likely show up at the bar as soon as they finished their visit with the kids from the Wishes Foundation. But he'd probably get at least an hour, maybe two, alone with Claire.

"No, that's fine. It is your birthday, after all. You get to call the shots today."

After the fastest shower he could manage while keeping his cast dry, he threw on cargo shorts and a T-shirt, and they were on their way.

The bar was dimly lit and half-empty. Claire settled next to him in the corner booth, close enough for him to drape his arm over her shoulder. When her margarita and his beer arrived, she lifted hers in toast. At her smile, the rest of the bar fell away. "Happy birthday, Liam."

He clinked their glasses together and then took a long swallow. "Thanks. It's turned out to be a good one."

She sipped her margarita. "I was impressed by your mad juggling skills earlier. Where did you learn to do that and the acrobatics?"

"When I ran away from home and joined the circus."

Gaping at him, she sputtered her sip then laughed as she wiped her mouth. "You did not."

"Okay, the real story is that I have an MFA in Ensemble Based Physical Theatre. And I learned how to juggle when I was in high school because I thought it looked cool." He shrugged and couldn't conceal his smile. The look on her face had been priceless. "See? Isn't the first answer more interesting?"

She shook her head. "The first answer is a typical Liam

response. The second one is surprising and a lot more interesting than my accounting degree."

"I can picture you behind a desk, crunching numbers. Sexy dark-framed glasses perched on your nose."

"I don't wear glasses."

"Hey, in my fantasy, you do."

Desire replaced the laughter, darkening her gaze. She licked at the salt on the rim of her glass. "Do you? Fantasize about me?"

His body heated and hardened just at the mention of the fantasy. "Do you like that? Knowing that I fantasize about you?" He molded his palm around her shoulder then gently stroked down her arm. "In my fantasy I kiss you. Like yesterday." He inched closer and leaned in. "I'd like to kiss you again."

She trailed her fingers along his forearm. A slow, deliberate touch that inflamed his desire. "Me too."

He brought his other hand up to frame her face. Fingers cold from the frosty beer warmed against her skin. When her tongue darted out to moisten her lips, he groaned and dove in, desperate for a taste. Salt and lime and a hint of sweetness.

Her short haircut left her delectable neck bare. He slid his hand along the tender column then cupped his hand behind her head to deepen their kiss.

Claire hummed her approval and tilted her head closer to his. Strands of hair tickled his hand. He ran his thumb along her neck and sucked in a breath when her hand slipped from his chest to his stomach.

Somewhere distant, a glass shattered. Slowly, the other sounds of the bar reemerged—music and people and conversations growing louder. Claire drew her hand away and Liam lifted his head. Blue eyes dazed with arousal stared into his and then she licked her lips like she was absorbing more of his taste. "We have an audience so we should probably talk about something else."

"Good idea." Lie. Such a lie. He captured her fingers and brought them to his lips. "Like what?"

She shivered, and then firmly pulled her hand away. "How about where to take Fin and Fiona next? We need to film more videos. How much longer will you be stuck in your cast?"

"Two weeks. I can't wait to ditch it. All of this hopping around and standing on one leg makes me feel like a cross between a rabbit and a flamingo."

Her laughter was music to his soul. He reached for his beer. Getting rid of the cast was the first step on his road back. But thinking too much about what would or could happen after he'd been cleared to return to his job soured the beer in his stomach. He pushed those thoughts away and focused on the beautiful blonde at his side. "Fin and Fiona left off after that kiss on the cheek."

Her eyes sparkled. "If we're plotting a romance, we need fuel. Let's get the loaded nachos, the quesadillas, and another drink."

"I'm on it." He raised his hand, catching their waiter's attention, then downed the rest of his beer.

His feelings about Claire were too ingrained in the what-if thoughts that lingered in the back of his mind like the threat of a storm on the horizon. He needed to be careful. Falling too hard wouldn't be smart. Not when the future was so up in the air.

Slade

After a full nine innings of a nail-biting, edge-of-your-seat, action-packed game, Slade was looking forward to unwinding by hanging out with Mason and the rest of the Wishes Granted patients. The smell of the grass, the breeze brushing his skin, and the peals of children's laughter coming from the field drained the stress from his system. Then, Savanna's laugh mixed in, dancing on the wind.

His muscles ached and his ribs hurt from getting hit by a pitch, but Savanna's presence dissipated his fatigue like magic and filled him with a mixture of contentment, energy and desire.

Carrying the Louisville Slugger he'd had specially made for Mason, engraved with the boy's name and designed for an eight-year-old to use, he wound his way through the dugout and onto the field.

Mason's face split into a grin. "Slade!"

His heart melted at the excited voice and the happiness sparking in the boy's eyes. "How are you doing, buddy?"

"Good." He wore the jersey and hat that Slade had gifted to him at the hospital. "I can't believe I get to have batting practice with you."

"Not just with me. My friend Adam is going to pitch to you and my friend Dom is going to play catch with whoever isn't batting." He'd requested permission for Mason and the kids to have a private, on-field batting practice after the game and the team had obliged. They rolled out the batting practice nets and let the kids take the field.

Mason stepped closer, hero-worship in his gaze. "Can you teach me how you hit a slider?"

Slade crouched until he was eye-level with the boy, and then he held out the bat. "I'll do my best. Maybe this will help. It's just like mine, only sized just right for you. It's yours to keep so you can practice whenever you want."

Mason's eyes widened like saucers. He traced his finger over his name with reverence. And then he launched himself into Slade and flung his thin arms around his neck. "Thank you."

Tears pricked his eyes as he patted Mason's back. "You got it, bud. Now let's see what you can do."

Adam and Dom joined them. While the kids crowded around the two ballplayers, Slade sought out Savanna. She laid her hand on his shoulder and pressed a kiss to his cheek. "You're a good guy."

Heat flushed through him and he shrugged to cover it. "He's too small to swing the bats we use."

"Don't worry, your secret is safe with me." She stepped back and let Mason lead him over to home plate.

For the next hour, he focused on instruction and encouragement, adjusted hand and foot positions, and how to eye the ball, but the true point was just spending time with the kids. He already had a soft spot for Mason and fell hard for his generous spirit when Mason made sure that all the kids took a turn batting with his new bat.

And then, the little boy twisted toward Savanna's perch by the dugout, holding out the bat. "Miss Savanna, you should take a turn too."

"No, that's all right, let one of the other kids take a turn." But she came closer.

"Everyone else already went."

Slade nodded at her. He wanted to see her in action. "Do it."

Mason glanced between them. "Slade helped me with my stance. He can help you too."

She gently tugged the bill of his cap and accepted the bat. Mason ran off to join the rest of the kids playing catch with Dom in the outfield, and Savanna eyed Slade with a smile. "I played summer softball on a rec league team when I was seven."

Slade squinted at her, seeing her in a whole new light. "You never told me that."

"I'd forgotten about it. I only played for one season. I think I remember how to bat." She gave him a teasing glimpse of skin when she stretched her arms over her head and then settled into a batter's stance at the plate.

Desire pounded through his blood as he moved closer. How could he get through the rest of the visit without touching her? "Too bad you know how to play."

She paused mid-swing, then rested the bat on her shoulder. Surprise colored her features. "Why?"

"If you didn't, I could do this." His arms covered hers, his hands cupped hers and he drew her back against his chest. "And use the excuse of showing you how to bat."

She turned her head and her perfume tempted him to lean in closer. "Why don't we pretend I need a refresher?"

Her soft lips brushed his jaw. Slade bent and hovered, taking in her features, the elegant brows, bewitching eyes, the slope of her nose and parted lips. "I think you're the one who's got the moves."

The desire to kiss her urged him forward. His lips closed over hers and his hand skimmed her silky skin, on a lingering journey from her hand to her cheek. A sigh escaped her lips. Her arms lowered and the bat hit the ground with a soft thud. Savanna shifted, angling her body toward him. Long, delicate fingers gripped his biceps.

"Hey you two, not in front of the kids." Adam's teasing voice carried from the pitcher's mound.

Slade tightened his grip and Savanna's lips curved against his. Then he lowered his arms and stepped away from her inviting heat. "Your stance looks good from where I'm standing."

"Your opinion might be slightly biased, but I'll take it." She picked up the bat and readied for Adam's pitch. Her Riptide T-shirt skimmed her curves and Slade's hands itched to get under it. Instead, he focused on her stance.

A strong, level swing, but she swung too early every time. "Take a step back. You're crowding the plate." He demonstrated, pleased when her next swing connected with the ball and it sailed toward Dom at center field. Dom made an exaggerated diving catch that cracked up the kids.

She glanced at her watch. "And on that note, it's time for us to get back."

Bedlam reigned as the kids gathered their things and made their goodbyes. Mason hugged Slade tight, and Slade promised to visit soon.

Soft fingers touched the back of his arm and Slade turned. Savanna held out her hand, offering a professional handshake as if they hadn't kissed in front of the kids already. "Thank you for making Mason's wish come true."

He brushed his hands up her arms, the caress quick, but burning into his fingertips. "I don't think I'll get to see you before we leave for our road trip on Thursday. We'll be gone for thirteen days, and then right back here with four home games."

Some of the light faded from her gaze. "So, three weeks then?"

"Three weeks." Which would feel like forever. The two weeks' wait between dates one and two had been tough. The ten days between their rock climbing adventure and today hadn't been much easier.

She linked their fingers together. "Call me from the road."

"I will." Too many pairs of curious eyes prevented him

from giving her anything more than a quick hug. He pulled back, unsatisfied, and strangely, missing her already.

Being with her soothed him on a cellular level. He couldn't explain it. In the short time they'd known each other, she'd become necessary, like a drug he'd gotten addicted to after taking only one hit. He didn't know what would happen if she threw him into a sudden detox.

CHAPTER TEN

CLAIRE

Claire adjusted her hold on the garment bags containing her and Liam's costumes and slowed her pace to match his plodding progress with the crutches. They navigated through the halls of Children's Hospital, having completed a successful visit. "Those kids loved the plush versions of Fin and Fiona."

Nodding, he concentrated on his path. "It's pretty cool seeing the stuffed animal of your character, isn't it?"

The Fiona merchandise, T-shirts and the plush animal, had arrived at the ballpark's fan shop right after Fin's birthday. Claire had purchased one of everything. "I liked how the last girl we saw asked why the stuffed version of Fin didn't have a cast."

He grunted and stopped to let a group of visitors pass. "One week to go until I can ditch this cast. I'm so ready. Showering is tough, not banging into things is tough. Not being able to carry a cup of coffee to the balcony is tough. I can't wait to be fully mobile."

They stepped outside into the late afternoon sunlight. She followed Liam to his car and laid his garment bag across his backseat. "Do you have plans tonight?"

"Just a regular Friday night of watching the game and having a beer. The guys play tonight at seven." He cocked his head to one side and a sly grin curved his lips. "So… Do you want to watch the game with me? It's good to keep an eye on what the other mascots in the league are doing. The guys will bring me back scouting reports though, if you want to do something else."

"Wait, scouting reports? Are you being serious or is this another joke?"

His eyes crinkled with his smile. "Not long, detailed handwritten notes, but they'll text me with the gist of the mascots' moves. We need to stay competitive."

"You do take this seriously."

"The fans pay a lot for tickets. They deserve the best performance we can give them."

She couldn't fault him there. "I'd love to watch the game with you."

He shifted closer, his chest grazing hers and igniting her desire. "Dinner too?"

"Dinner would be good." Her body heated and she stretched onto her toes to meet his waiting lips.

Her phone vibrated in her back pocket. She eased away from Liam and reached for it. Lauren's number, calling not texting. Lauren always communicated via text.

"Let me grab this." She slid her thumb across the screen. "Hello?"

"I fell off the balance beam and rolled my ankle. It really hurts. Coach Kay thinks I sprained it, but what if I broke it?" Short sniffs mixed in with her words. No doubt, Lauren was crying.

Desire and duty twisted up inside her. She loved her sister deeply and sympathized, having been down the road of injury and disappointment many times. "Break would be better. You'd heal faster. Where are you now?"

"At the gym. It just happened. Can you please come?"

"Did you call Dad?"

"No." She sniffed again. "He's at work."

"I'm on my way. We'll go to urgent care and get you an x-ray." She ended the call, left a voice mail for her dad, and then turned to Liam. "I'm sorry. I need to leave."

"I heard." His lips pressed into a forced grin and he looked down at his cast. "Totally get it. I hope she'll be okay. Do you want me to come in case you need help?"

She blinked at his words, unsure if she'd heard him correctly. "Really?"

He nodded at his crutches with a self-deprecating shrug. "I can't help carry her or go on a coffee run for you if there's a long wait, but I can sit there and tell her stupid shark jokes, and we can compare injuries."

"I'd like that." She kissed him again, appreciative and amazed. She'd never really had anyone to lean on.

Two hours later, she led Lauren and Liam into her family home, then helped Lauren get settled on the couch in the living room. She shook her head at the soda cans, books, and magazines that littered the coffee table. "I'll get some pillows so you can elevate your ankle."

"Can I have a blanket and some iced tea too?"

"Sure."

When she returned with the pillows and blanket, Lauren was taking a photo of her ankle. Her sister twisted toward where Liam sat in the armchair and held out her phone. "Which filter makes my injury look more dramatic?"

The corner of his mouth winged up in a smile. "I like the third one, where everything in the background fades out. But..." He pushed to standing and hobbled over. Leaning on his crutches, he took her phone and then captured another photo. "This one includes your crutches in the shot."

"Ooh, that's better. Thanks." Lauren accepted her phone and winced as Claire set the pillows under her bandaged ankle. "Maybe I should take another picture with the pillows."

Claire paused in gathering the empty cans. "Why do you need so many photos?"

"I have to see the best one to put on social media. My friends will want to know how I'm doing." She flipped her hair over her shoulder and frowned at her ankle. "I don't know how I'll handle getting around school next week."

Rolling her eyes at the dramatics, Claire tossed the cans into the recycle bin. Could her sister have actually forgotten the doctor's instructions so quickly? She sighed at the sink full of dishes. Who knew if her sisters had worked out a new chore system? There wasn't any evidence of one in the kitchen. She grabbed an ice pack and the glass of tea and delivered them to her sister with two pain pills. "It's a mild sprain. Remember, the doctor said you'll be able to start putting weight on your ankle on Sunday. And you won't need the elastic bandage past Sunday or Monday. As long as you use the crutches, you'll be fine."

"Still. I'll need someone to help carry my books."

"You'll probably be okay using your backpack."

"Nope. I'll be off balance." Lauren again turned to Liam. "You understand, right? You told me all those stories in the waiting room about how it's been hard to get around. Maybe I need a golf cart too."

"Oh my god." Claire pinched the bridge of her nose. "You don't need a golf cart. You're going to be fine in a week. And until then, you have Krissy, Ginger, Amanda, Jen, and Dad to help you do things around here."

Lauren pouted and crossed her arms over her chest. "You don't have to get mad. I didn't get hurt on purpose."

Anger tingled on the edges of Claire's nerves. She'd had about all the teenage drama from Lauren she could tolerate for one evening. But losing her cool would only spoil her great day. She counted to ten. "I'm sorry. I know. I sent Dad a text with all the info the doctor gave me. He said he's going to try to come home early tonight if he can."

"Yeah, he sent me a text too." She looked at her phone again. "Krissy and Ginger are staying at a friend's house tonight, and Amanda and Jen won't be home until late. Can you stay until someone gets home?"

"Uh…sure." Claire met Liam's gaze. Definitely not how she'd thought the evening would turn out, but if her sister needed her, she couldn't leave.

He moved closer to her. "We missed dinner. Are you guys hungry? I can order something."

"Pizza and chocolate chip cookies," Lauren called from the couch. "Please? It would help me feel better."

He grinned and nodded. "Claire?"

"Anything's fine." She studied his gaze, trying to see past the smile. Was he intending to stay the whole evening with her? He'd seemed to take their change of plans in stride.

He made the call, and then dropped into her father's worn out recliner, chucking his crutches to the floor with a clank. The reach of his hand toward her convinced Claire to abandon straightening up her sisters' clutter and join him on the chair. She carefully sat by his side, conscious of his ankle and her sister's scrutiny.

He joked with Lauren until the food arrived, and after dinner, insisted on helping Claire clean up the evidence of their meal.

Later, as a movie played on the TV and they shared the

recliner, Claire leaned into Liam's strong fingers massaging the back of her neck. "I'm sorry tonight didn't go as planned, but thank you for being here."

"I'm sorry your sister is hurt, but I had fun. Is Lauren the one who texts you all the time?"

She glanced at her sister sleeping on the couch beside them. "Yeah. She really is a good kid, just dramatic."

"You mentioned your dad and your sisters, but not your mom. Is she…?"

"She isn't a part of our lives. Hasn't been for fifteen years. Her choice." She'd grown accustomed to stating the story matter-of-fact. Without emotion. Bitterness and anger depleted long ago after she'd realized those emotions only served to hurt her. Forgiving her mom then letting her go had allowed Claire to heal.

"I'm sorry."

"It's all right. I did the best I could to make up for her not being here. Even if we fight sometimes, my sisters know I'll always be there if they need me."

"Sounds like they rely on you a lot."

"For a long time they did, but only Lauren really does now. The others are a little older. The twins are seventeen, Jen's nineteen, and Amanda is twenty." She leaned her head on his shoulder. "I'd do anything for them, but I really enjoy waking up in my own apartment now and not have to worry about anyone but me. Oh god, that sounded selfish."

"No, it sounded honest. It's not selfish to live your own life. You've missed out on a lot playing mommy since you were a kid. Time they became as self-sufficient as you are. And time for you to have some fun." He shifted his hand into her hair. "I'm always ready to have fun. So, you know, we should have fun together."

"I like the sound of that." She needed someone like Liam

in her life. A born entertainer, an unending stream of jokes and laughter followed in his wake. So did a sense of joy. He was intuitive and caring. She loved the way he melted for the kids. And how the fiercely passionate man called to her on every level.

Yes. Just the man she needed—just the man she wanted.

For now.

She'd never wind up like her dad. Never test the strength of a promise.

CHAPTER ELEVEN

SLADE

There wasn't anything like flying. Or skydiving. The plane's door opened and Slade made his way to the back. He stepped to the edge and stared at the earth thirteen thousand feet below. With a grin, he gave the pilot a thumbs-up and jumped into the air. The first minute of free falling was an intense rush. His heartbeat thundered and adrenaline coursed through his veins, but after the parachute opened, the flight was quiet and inspiring. Nothing but the sky above him and the mountains below him. Seven glorious minutes where he could just *be*.

He'd had a decent game to start off the road trip last night, going three for four in his at-bats, including a walk-off home run in the ninth inning that helped his team win the game, but he hadn't seen Savanna in six days, hadn't spoken to his sister in a week, and still had no idea when his birth parents could meet him. The restlessness in his soul rattled loud and constant.

Which was why he'd woken up early, sneaked out of the team hotel, and spent the morning airborne.

Too soon, his boots touched the ground. He came in soft,

probably the best landing he'd ever done. After releasing himself from his parachute, he made his way to where Dom stood outside the canopied waiting area.

Most of his teammates had their own hotel room during road trips but Dom had always insisted that he liked having the company of a roommate and Slade gladly agreed, even though he suspected Dom pretended for his benefit. The older brother he'd never had, Dom gave him the stability of family, and was usually more than willing to accompany him on his adventures—from midnight pizza to keeping him company during the half hour drive to the skydiving facility and back.

Dom held up his phone, showing a video of the landing. "Nice job. I sent it to Liam. You about ready to head back? We'll have time to eat lunch with Adam and Gemma before heading over to the ballpark."

"Let's go." He liked that Dom didn't push him to talk, but was simply there, always there, when Slade needed him.

Five hours later, as his sat in the visitors' locker room after batting practice, he wished he could say the same for his team's manager.

Dusty Martin, Slade's candidate for Asshat of the Year, bellowed his name from the opposite side of the room. "Mac-Innes, what's this I hear about you skydiving?"

Slade cocked his head to the side. "What did you hear?"

Glowering at him, Dusty cut a path straight toward his locker. "That you spent the morning doing it. Skydiving's not going to fly. Not if you want to remain on my team."

Slade couldn't help the twitching of his lips. Dusty had just told him that *skydiving* wasn't going to *fly*. "You can't cut me for doing things on my own time."

"Think not?"

"I'm not violating anything in my contract."

Arms crossed and legs splayed wide, his manager

sneered. "That contract's going away. The team is working on your *next* contract and you can sure as shit expect language forbidding you from engaging in dangerous activities in there this time around."

"What the hell?" Slade surged to his feet, fists clenched. No one told him how to live his life. Dom's hand tugged on the back of his jersey but Slade didn't budge.

"*My* team works *my* way." Dusty thumped his fist against his chest in emphasis. "When you signed your last contract, no one knew about your penchant for reckless behavior. I won't have that kind of risk hanging over my team."

"I've never been reckless. The activities I do actually help me to be more focused on the field. I think my performance there speaks for itself. If you're worried about injuries, more happen on the field than off. Maybe we should start wearing bubble wrap under our uniforms."

The old man's face reddened and his eyes could have shot daggers. "You're not irreplaceable. Remember that."

Dusty swaggered away.

"Fucking tyrant," Slade muttered.

Fortunately, his manager couldn't hear him. He was too busy yelling at the relief pitchers for goofing off too much in the bullpen last night.

Dom's elbow connected hard with Slade's ribs. "Watch yourself. He's not above having you ride the bench for the rest of the season."

Rubbing his side, Slade sank into his seat and glared at Dom. "I'd like to see him try. The fans would have a fit."

"He'll spin it so they'll be ticked off at you for not being able to put your team first."

"Not put the team first? Is that what you really think of me?" Slade fought through the red haze of anger.

"Hell, no. You know that. But don't forget, I have experience in being his target." Dom squinted one eye and furrowed his brows then planted a heavy hand on Slade's shoulder. "I get that you need to blow off steam. I don't think any player on this team doubts that you put the team first."

"Good."

Dom held up his hand. "But if you get hurt and it's not a baseball-related injury, the team doesn't have to pay you like they would if you got hurt in a game. And if you're hurt bad enough, you might not make it to your next contract."

"Yeah." That would suck. But not enough to make him stop. He wouldn't live his life confined by maybes and what ifs.

"If they do bench you, the bad press could make other teams less likely to want to sign you. You'd be labeled too big a risk. I've seen it happen. Remember that rookie who couldn't stop partying no matter how many times the team gave him chances and ultimatums? He's not playing for anyone now and he's only twenty-three. Played ball his whole life and his career is in the toilet because of his choices off the field."

"Whoa." Slade shook his head vehemently. "That's not going to happen to me."

"I hope not, and you know I'd go to bat for you with anything. But just be careful."

"I'm always careful. I don't take stupid chances."

"Maybe you should lay off the adrenaline junkie activities until after the season's over."

"No freaking way." He resisted that suggestion all the way down to the marrow of his bones. Those experiences filled him in a way he needed. He simply wasn't sure of any other way to keep himself from imploding.

Dom nudged his shoulder until Slade met his gaze. His

dark eyes were serious. "I get why you need to do them. I'm suggesting you find an alternative."

Slade's shoulders sank. "What if there isn't an alternative?"

"Then we'll get you that virtual reality headset and you can go on any adventure you want from the safety of your own apartment."

"You mean the thing we saw in the infomercial last night? Turning geek on me?"

"Fuck off." Laughing, Dom chucked a handful of sunflowers seeds at his head. Slade ducked but not fast enough to avoid getting hit. "It's worth a try."

"I don't know, man. I guess."

"Or what about Savanna? You've been spending a lot of time with her."

"Yeah, doing things that Dusty probably wants to include on his list of fun activities to avoid."

"Rock climbing at a gym is probably on the safe list."

Slade snorted. Not the way he did it. "She didn't like climbing that much. She liked the hot air balloon ride though. And I know she likes my bike." He shot a glance around the room, making sure Dusty was gone. "I'm not giving up that bike, Dom."

"I hope not. I helped you pick out a great one."

"Dusty can suck it. I'm not signing any contract I don't agree with either."

"Then lay low for a while and let him get fixated on someone else so he forgets about giving his suggestions to the front office."

Slade leaned his head against the wall. Laying low made sense. He didn't want problems with the team, didn't want to be released, picked up or traded away from Dom and Liam and Adam. Forming those relationships, trusting those guys, had taken a long time. "I'll try, but I can't make any guarantees."

"Then it's a good thing I'm here with you twenty-four-seven for the next two weeks. I'll help."

Dom would. Dom always did.

Slade's phone vibrated on the bench. He picked it up, expecting to see Liam's name.

Savanna: Good luck tonight.

He kept staring at the screen. Three little words, but damn, they were enough to completely brighten his day.

Dom tapped his arm. "What's up? You're grinning like someone just told you Dusty got fired."

"That would be a reason to celebrate." He twisted his wrist and flashed the screen of his cell phone. "Savanna sent a text."

Dom's lips quirked in a smile and he patted Slade on the back. "I like her. She's good for you. Don't worry, I'm not going to hover. I'll go and bother Adam."

Slade hunched over his phone, thumbs over the keypad.

Slade: Hi.

He backed that out and started over.

Slade: Thanks.

Then he added *Miss you.*

No, that would be too much, too soon. He'd only been gone for six days. He moved his finger to the delete key but it brushed Send.

The sent message bubble popped onto the screen. Out there. For her to see.

Shit. Shit. Shit.

Miss you would come across as too intense. Even if it was true.

Maybe he could blame auto-correct… But as a correction for what?

"MacInnes!" Dusty barked from the doorway. "Let's move it."

His teammates were leaving, headed onto the field for warm ups. He threw his phone into his locker. For the next few hours, he needed to put the text out of his mind and concentrate on the upcoming game.

But as he ran onto the field, he knew he'd probably get distracted wondering how she'd react.

Liam

Liam sat on the exam table in the training room, staring at his ankle as Andy used a rotary saw to remove his cast. He couldn't wait to be free. The countdown to cast removal had begun the day he'd had the thing put on. Six long weeks of awkward mobility and limited abilities and inconveniencing those around him.

The cast and wrappings removed, his foot, ankle, and leg were swollen and blotchy. "Is it supposed to look like that?"

"Totally normal. No need to worry. In a few days, the color should return to normal and the swelling in your leg and toes should decrease, but your ankle and foot will be swollen for a while."

"All right." He grabbed his phone and sent a picture of his leg to Slade, Dom, and Adam. They'd been gone for a week and still had a week to go in the road trip. He missed his friends.

Slade's response was a series of emojis starting with a thumbs-up and happy face and ending with a puking one.

Andy held up a black boot constructed of a hard shell with a soft inner area and Velcro straps. "You can start putting partial pressure on your foot since the bones looked good but I want you to wear this for two weeks. It provides support to the healing ankle."

"By putting pressure on my foot, do you mean actual walking around?"

"Yes, start putting one foot in front of the other while using the crutches and wearing the boot." Andy narrowed his eyes. "I know you, Liam. Don't overdo it. If you push too hard, you're going to end up injuring the ankle again. You haven't used the muscles or tendons for a while, so it's going to ache and be swollen."

He could deal with achy and swollen. "When do you think I'll be back to my usual antics?"

"It depends. If the swelling decreases enough that you can put on a sneaker when I see you in two weeks, you can get started with physical therapy then. If not, it'll mean a few more weeks in the boot. I'll evaluate you again after six weeks of therapy to test your readiness to return to the job. But a return to full participation in sports and work activities generally occurs twelve to sixteen weeks after an ankle fracture, so don't get your hopes up if at the end of June, I still think you need another month or so of therapy."

"Got it, doc. But there's a good chance I could be back to normal by the All-Star break, right?"

Andy sighed. "Liam. I'm thrilled that you've been taking recovery so seriously, but you can't rush it. Doing so would be a mistake that you'd pay for a long time. Remember, when the injury happened, I cautioned that it could take months for you to regain full strength and range of motion."

"I know. I know." He didn't want to hear about that again. Any timetable greater than the All-Star game in mid-July was unacceptable. With the Riptide hosting the game, the team wanted to do everything possible to ensure a successful fan experience. And that included having Liam back and at his best.

"Some patients have weakness and mobility issues for up to two years after a bad break."

Stop, stop, stop. The very idea turned his stomach. "But this wasn't a bad break, Andy. I can't take two years to get back to normal. The team won't let me keep my job that long if I can't do it. They'd replace me."

"We don't know what's going to happen. The ankle is healing well, but you're not returning to a desk job. You're returning to a physically demanding one that will test your ankle with every move you make. All I'm saying is that we need to be cautious, but I hope you'll be back on the field by the middle of July."

"I'll do whatever it takes to make that happen."

"I know you will. My concern is that you'll overdo it." Andy set his foot in the boot and tightened the straps. "Take the boot off two or three times a day to ice the ankle."

"Yes, sir."

"Okay, let's see you stand on it."

Liam swallowed the fear that the ankle would snap again and he'd go down. Andy held out his crutches. He grabbed them and eased off the table. His ankle hurt. He took a tentative step. The sole and heel of his foot tingled, like little electrical pinpoints.

"Looking good. How does it feel?"

"Great." Liam pasted on a smile.

"So, in other words, it hurts." Andy shook his head. "Liam, I'm honest with you. You need to be honest with me. I'm on your side here."

"I know. And you're right, it's sore and my foot is tingly."

"That part will go away in a few days."

"Okay, cool." He walked carefully, using the crutches to support his weight. "Am I free to go now, Doc?"

"I'll see you in two weeks. Stop in or call if you need me."

Liam shook his hand and then began the slow journey down the hall.

If he didn't heal properly or fast enough, he wouldn't be able to keep his job. What the hell else was he going to do? For the first time, he regretted his theater degree. Maybe he should've chosen something as normal and boring as Claire had with accounting. Where else besides being a mascot would acrobatics and juggling be marketable skills? Maybe he'd have to end up running away and joining the circus after all.

Laughing at the thought, he climbed into the golf cart and headed to his office.

Claire was there, pulling on her costume when he arrived. "Hey, you got your cast off. Whoa, and you're walking. That's great."

"Yep. Andy says it's healing well." He picked up his costume from where she'd laid it on the couch. "A few weeks with the boot and crutches, and then we'll evaluate it again."

They filmed videos of Fin surprising Fiona with a huge bouquet of flowers in the clubhouse, one with them sitting in two seats in the stadium with his fin on top of hers and her head on his shoulder, and one with them at a table together for their first date, complete with candlelight.

They covered one end of the stadium to the other. By the time they finished the last video, Liam's ankle ached like someone had shoved a screwdriver into it. He needed pain meds, ice, and elevation.

Claire drove the golf cart back to the office. "Are you okay? You've been quiet."

Grimacing at the ache, he grabbed his crutches and climbed out of the cart. "We can't talk in the videos."

"I know that, silly." She unlocked the door and held it open for him to pass through. "But you were quiet in between filming too, and you're never quiet then."

He pulled off his mask. Sitting on the edge of his desk, he reached for his zipper. "I might have overdone it with the walking."

"Oh, Liam." Claire slipped out of her costume, then helped him remove his. "What can I do?"

"Nurse Fiona would probably yell at Fin. I'm hoping you won't do that."

Face pinched in concern, she ran her hands over his shoulders. "Do you need me to get you some pain meds?"

"Thanks, but I have everything I need at home. I'm glad we're done for the day."

Her capable hands massaged his shoulders. "I can go with you, help you get settled with ice and food so all you need to do is stay off your foot."

"That falls under work and not having fun. I can't ask you to take care of me."

"You're not asking. I'm offering."

He leaned down until their foreheads rested against each other. "You got stuck taking care of Lauren all of last weekend. You're supposed to be having fun with me, not playing Florence Nightingale."

"I'm sure you'll be less of a drama queen than my sister. And I always have fun with you. Tonight, we can watch the game together and you can show me how you evaluate mascots."

"That would be nice." Who was he kidding, it would be amazing.

"I'll follow you to your place."

The drive to his apartment took longer than usual, but with seeing Claire in his rear view mirror the entire time, he didn't mind. He pointed out the restaurant while they waited for the elevator. "We can order something from there or get whatever you want."

"Do you have any food in your apartment?"

"Sure. But I don't think I can hobble around the kitchen, cooking tonight."

She guided him into the elevator. "I can. Which floor?"

"Seventeen."

When they stepped inside his apartment, she closed the door then inspected his space with a grin and a surprised nod. "Nice place."

He thought so or at least he used to. Since living a life on crutches, he'd started to consider the apartment too big. The rooms he used seem far apart when his arms ached from supporting most of his weight. Finally healing and returning to his old routine couldn't come fast enough. "Come in. Make yourself at home. Can I get you something to drink?"

"You need to get your foot elevated. As long as you don't mind my poking around your kitchen, you should get settled on the couch and I'll bring you some ice."

"Poke away." He made it into the living room then collapsed onto the couch before swinging his bum leg onto the ottoman for a full length stretch. Getting off his feet felt so good. Two decorative pillows were within reach. He shoved them under his foot, then reached down again and removed the boot.

His sock had grown snug and his foot more swollen that it had been in Andy's office. Closing his eyes, he leaned his head back on the cushion. Though relieved to be cast-free, disappointment harshened his mood. He'd thought once the cast came off, he'd feel like his old self. He didn't. Not even close.

Soft footsteps announced Claire's entry. He opened his eyes. She looked like an angel with her shining hair and sympathetic gaze as she laid the ice pack across his ankle and adjusted his pillows. "I found fresh pasta in the fridge."

"Sounds good." He clasped her hand. "Thank you."

A few minutes later, she brought the bowl of pasta, a glass of water, and pain relievers. He waited until she'd joined him with her own meal, and then turned on the TV. Seeing his friends on the screen—Dom at center field, Slade at first base, and Adam on the pitcher's mound—made him smile. It was almost as good as having them in the room with him. When the camera panned to Dusty leaning against the dugout's fence, Liam launched into a few stories about the grumpy old man, his personal run-ins and stories the guys had shared over beers. Making Claire laugh was a small payment for all the kindness she'd shown him.

Claire set their empty bowls on the coffee table and then leaned against his shoulder. "How's your ankle feeling?"

"The ice is helping a lot." He slid his arm around her shoulders. "Having you here is helping a lot too."

She rewarded him with a smile. "Yeah?"

"Yeah."

"Good." She snuggled into his side. "Now, show me what we should be looking for when evaluating the competition."

CHAPTER TWELVE

SAVANNA

Miss you.

The text had stayed on her mind for two weeks. Savanna washed the lunch dishes and brewed a pot of coffee for her parents, counting down the hours until Slade would arrive.

He hadn't mentioned the text either of the times they'd spoken during his road trip. Or when he'd called her last night to confirm plans for their date. She hadn't mentioned it either. But she'd missed him too. Three weeks was a long time to be apart.

She carried the cups and carafe into the living room and set the tray on her coffee table. "Here you go."

Her mom pointed to the TV, where the Riptide game was in the middle of the fifth inning. "You're going on a date with that man?"

"I've been on a few dates with him already."

"But how do you know he's a good man? You can't trust these superstars."

"You're generalizing, Mom. I've known him for three years. He does a lot of work with the kids in the foundation."

"Hmm." Mom poured coffee, then handed Savanna one of the steaming cups. "Careful, it's hot."

She bit back her response that yes, she could see the steam rising from the cup the same way she'd held in her retort when her mother had cautioned about the knife's sharpness while Savanna had sliced strawberries earlier.

Dad reached for the creamer. "Where is he taking you?"

"I don't know yet. It's a surprise." Again, Slade had told her to dress casually. Her shorts, blouse, and sandals fit that description.

On screen, the camera zoomed in to a close-up of Slade, his face lit in a grin, laughing at something one of his teammates said. His stats were displayed across the bottom of the screen.

Mom sighed. "Well, what is he like?"

"He's kind. Generous. Adventurous."

Dad frowned and held out his phone. Photos of Slade filled the screen. "He's a thrill-seeker. I typed in his name and there's as many photos of him doing something dangerous as there are of him on the baseball field."

"Savanna." Mom set her cup down. "You shouldn't get involved with a man like that. He'll end up getting you killed."

She huffed out a breath and stared at the ceiling, cursing herself for ever mentioning that she was dating Slade. "He's not reckless. He's very… careful with me. We've gone for a hot-air balloon ride and indoor rock climbing."

Mom squeezed her eyes closed and massaged her forehead with all ten fingers. "I'm going to worry about you tonight, not knowing where you are or what you're doing. You better call me when you get home."

"I'm not a kid. I can take care of myself."

"Not if you get injured. Look, there he is inside a race car.

You can't take care of yourself if you hit a wall at two hundred miles an hour."

Oh. My. God. Shaking her head, she stalked to the window. "I wouldn't go zooming around a track at that speed. He knows that. You're being crazy and not giving me enough credit."

"I'm not crazy for caring about you. What do his parents think of him doing these things? Do they approve?" Mom matched her temper for temper.

But at the mention of his parents, Savanna's anger faded. "He doesn't have any. He was adopted as a baby and didn't have a good home life. I think it was actually pretty bad."

The fire sparking in her mother's eyes fizzled and her face creased in concern. "That poor boy."

"I know." She sighed and then gave her mom a hug. "You guys can stick around and meet him if that'll make you feel better, but don't say anything about what I told you."

The game ended at three-thirty, and at four-thirty, Slade knocked on her door. She didn't hear the motorcycle's roar, so he must have driven his car. Her dad let him in before she could and she inwardly cringed as introductions were made, but her parents refrained from saying anything about his "thrill-seeking."

Slade kissed her cheek, dressed just as casually in shorts, a T-shirt, and sneakers. "Are you ready to go? We have a half hour drive and we don't want to miss our reservation."

Mom stepped closer to Savanna and cast Slade a distrustful glance. "Where are you going?"

"Para-sailing in Marina del Rey."

Savanna opened her mouth, but her dad spoke first. "Isn't that a little dangerous?"

Slade met Savanna's gaze before turning to address her father. "Not at all. It's one of the safest water sports. The place we're going has highly trained, certified, licensed captains and crew members. I wouldn't take any risks with Savanna."

She slid her hand into his. "We should go. Mom and Dad, thanks for coming over. I'll call you this week."

"Call us tonight so we know you got home safe."

Heat flushed into Savanna's cheeks. "I can't promise I'll remember to call. I'll try to remember to text, okay? Don't worry so much."

She hugged them both, and then they shook hands with Slade. Her dad turned back once on his way to his car. "Be careful."

Slade nodded. "I'll always keep Savanna safe."

She waved him inside and closed the door. "I'll just be a minute. I need to get my—"

He pulled her into his arms and his mouth descended, hard and hungry, covering hers, coaxing it open. One hand fisted in her hair, and the other splayed wide across her low back. He drew her lower lip into his mouth, grazing it with his teeth before caressing it with his tongue.

Her right hand, trapped between them, clutched at his shirt. She slid her other hand around his back and held tight.

His fingers trailed up her spine, setting off a series of tingles. "Missed you."

She felt the murmur against her lips, tasted how much, and freed her mouth enough to whisper, "Me too" before drawing him to her once again. He smelled like soap and cologne and tasted like mint and magic.

With a low groan, he lifted his head. "We need to leave if we don't want to miss our reservation. But if you want to skip it and stay here…"

"Did you have to pay ahead of time?"

"Yeah. But don't worry about that."

"No. We'll go." Even as she drew away, happiness at seeing him burst out of her as bright as sunlight. She couldn't stop smiling. "I'll get my purse."

An hour later, fitted with life jackets and harnesses, they sat next to each other on the flight deck of a private boat in the ocean awaiting lift-off. Slade grasped her hand. "How are you doing?"

"Pretty good. A little nervous. I'm sure you can tell my palms are sweating. The harness is like being strapped into a swing, but I feel like we're waiting for a roller coaster to make its first big drop."

His eyebrows rose. "You like roller coasters?"

"Um, no. Not really."

"Why not?"

"The danger of falling out. I know it doesn't happen often, but it does happen."

His thumb stroked the back of her hand. "Well, this is nothing like that. Take off is very slow and gentle. The whole experience should be peaceful, like floating."

"Peaceful and floating sound good." The captain had assured her that the rope wouldn't break, that they were in good hands. He'd promised the views from the air were amazing, and she tried to concentrate on that and nothing else.

And then they were moving, lifted up as the boat pulled out in front of them. She tightened her grip on Slade's hand. They hovered close to the water and then gently rose, higher and higher, until the boat was as tiny as a toy. Her body dipped back and forth, swaying like she was on an actual swing.

Overhead, the colorful parachute in a rainbow design sheltered them from the sun, and her breath caught at the beautiful panoramic views of Santa Monica Bay. "Thank you for thinking of this. I love it."

"I hoped you would. I'm glad you were free today. I didn't want to have to wait to see you."

"Me either. I know you don't have a game tomorrow. Do you have anything planned?" She could probably leave work at five and meet him for dinner.

He pulled off his sunglasses and tucked them into the collar of his T-shirt. A series of emotions—worry, hope, fear, and pain—flickered over his face. "I'm meeting my birth parents tomorrow night."

Thrilled for him, she twisted to give him a hug only to meet the resistance of the harness. "That's... wow. Are you ready? Nervous? Excited? Never mind, you're probably all of those things."

"Those, and a few more. I don't know how it's going to go." He squeezed her hand like he sought reassurance.

She squeezed back, then brought her other hand over to cover his on both sides. "I hope the meeting will be exactly what you need it to be."

"Me too." He averted his attention to the scenery, but she noticed the tension in his jaw.

"Call me if you what to talk about it, before or after, or both."

"I'll let you know what happens."

Needing to make him smile and lighten the mood, she tapped his foot with hers and gestured to the view. "This really is nice, like we're floating on air."

"It reminds me of the feeling I get when I'm skydiving. The slow float down is like this."

A tendril of trepidation teased through her stomach. Was he hinting at their next adventure? "I don't think I could ever do that."

"Skydiving? Sure you could. But I'm not going to force you. If you ever wanted to do it, I'd be right there. But if you don't, you don't." He raised her hand to his lips and kissed her fingers.

Still, there was a hard line dividing the things she'd be willing to try and the things there was no way in hell she'd do. They needed to have a discussion. But not while they were in the middle of such a lovely experience, and not during the first time they'd seen each other in three weeks. There would be time for that later.

Coming in for the landing was as gentle as going up had been. They slowly descended and landed softly on their feet, standing up. After they'd been unhooked from the chute and had shed their harnesses and life jackets, they stood together, looking out over the water as the boat cut through the water on its way to the pier.

Savanna leaned against Slade's side. He wrapped his arm around her back and his hand stroked over her hip. She snuggled closer. "I really liked this."

"I'm glad. Maybe you should call your mom now and let her know you survived." He smiled, but didn't appear to be teasing.

"If I do, she'll want another call once I'm safely in my apartment, so I'll wait on that. She worries a lot."

He kissed her temple. "Mmm hmm. I guess that's where you get it."

"What?" Torn between surprise, insult, and annoyance, she pulled away from him. "I'm not like her. I know I worry, but I'm not as bad as she is. She worries about *everything*, including a lot of little things that don't bother me."

Slade studied her a moment and then looked out at the horizon. "Let me ask you something. Was she always the way she is now?"

Pressing her lips together, Savanna thought back over the years. "She was overprotective when I was a kid, but not this bad. She went off the deep end with the worrying after my sister died. Dad did too, but to a lesser degree. I guess they were both so worried about losing me after they'd lost Molly."

He linked their fingers together. "Is that when you started worrying and became more cautious too?"

"I never really worried about something happening to either of them. I always assumed they'd be there. But it makes sense that being told over and over that everything in the world had the potential to hurt me probably is why I'm the way I am. But changing that way of thinking is so, so hard." She sighed and leaned on the rail. "I'm a mess."

"You're not a mess." He drew her close once again.

"I just need my brain rewired."

"Well, when you kiss me, my circuits short out." His hand teased into her hair and drew it away from her face.

Her heart warmed at his confession. She lifted her face to his, wanting a kiss, and he didn't disappoint. Wrapping her arms around his waist, she gave herself over to the sensations of being in Slade's arms. The thrill of the thrill-seeker had only grown stronger, and for the moment, she didn't worry about anything. Slade filled her senses, and when that happened, she stopped being afraid.

Slade

He'd been on edge all day, but as the miles and minutes to his meeting with his birth parents evaporated, Slade's stomach was a tangled knot of nerves that swelled so big, he wanted to claw out of his skin. Drumming his hands on the dashboard and shifting in his seat didn't help rid his system of the jangling energy. There was no way he could have driven, not with his mind flipping between old memories and the uncertainty of the future. Thankfully, Liam had volunteered.

Maybe this was something he was supposed to do on his own, but he needed Liam there. "Thanks for driving, and you know, being here."

Liam turned the steering wheel in a smooth move and then his gaze flicked to Slade. "Anytime. This is their street. Are you ready?"

"Yes and no."

They pulled into the driveway of a modest split-level brick home that had a rock garden and pink flowers in yellow window boxes.

Slade breathed in deep. Once. Twice. Then Liam's hand touched his shoulder. "Dude, they're going to be ecstatic. I'll be right here if you need me."

Slade nodded and climbed out of the car. His heart thudded hard, like a fist punching into a baseball glove.

The front door opened before he reached it. Melanie beamed a smile. "You're here. Come in. Mom and James are in the family room. They're pretty nervous. I told them I'd let you in, in case you were nervous too." She led Slade into the foyer and toward a wide archway. "Here we are. I'll give you privacy."

The couple sitting together, holding hands on the couch under a large bay window, rose to their feet. Slade shuffled into the room. He had his dad's tall build and blue eyes. "Hi."

"Slade." Tears in her eyes, Tiffany reached out her hands. "May we hug you?"

Choked up, all he could do was nod and spread his arms wide. She hugged him tight, and then James put his arms around them both. Tiffany's shoulders shook and the front of Slade's shirt grew damp. He returned the hug, unsure of what he should be feeling. They were strangers, and yet, they weren't.

Sniffling, she eased back and with a watery laugh, brushed at the evidence of her tears. "I'm so happy to meet you."

"Me too." James wiped at his eyes and stepped away. "Please, sit."

Slade chose the chair beside the couch. He couldn't stop looking at them, searching for more similarities, the shape of a chin, their hands, their mannerisms.

Tiffany grasped James' hand. "I thought about you every day. Every single day."

"Knowing that a part of me was out there somewhere in the world and I'd likely never see you again." James' voice cracked and he shook his head. "I made a decision at sixteen that I've regretted so much over the years. I've pictured you in every possible job, wondered about who you were, what you'd become."

Slade swallowed against a thickening throat. "I wondered about you guys too."

"We'll tell you anything you want to know."

He took a deep breath, and then asked the one question he had asked himself the most. "Why did you give me up?"

Face flushed, Tiffany glanced at James and swallowed hard. He nodded at his wife and let go of her hand. She scooted toward Slade, but stayed on the couch. Her foot tapped in a restless rhythm that matched his perfectly. Same foot and everything. "We were too young. You have to understand, I was raised in a chaotic home, not a loving one. They didn't support my decision to keep you. The fights were nothing less than traumatic. Dad said if I wanted to have the baby to go ahead, but not under his roof. I didn't have much choice. I had nowhere else to go. Honestly, I didn't want to raise my child in that environment anyway. I wanted better for you."

James cleared his throat. "I thought adoption would give you a chance at a good life. I was immature. I didn't know how to be a dad at that age and I was too scared to try."

Slade nodded. He could understand. They'd been too young. He couldn't fault them for doing what they'd thought was the best thing for him. He might have done the same thing at their age. They hadn't hated him, as he'd feared. They'd struggled hard with their decision. "Did you get to pick out Jeannette, the woman who adopted me?"

"They didn't give us any information about her, other than she was a relative of someone who attended the same church as my parents, and she couldn't have kids." The tension in Tiffany's voice reflected his own. "When Melanie told us that she'd found you, and then who you were, we couldn't believe it. We've seen you play ball, but that's all we know about you."

"Please," James moved closer to his wife and leaned forward to rest his elbows on his thighs, "tell us about you. We want to know everything."

"Well…" he hesitated only long enough to take a deep breath then the words flowed easier than he expected. "I grew up in Malibu. Jeannette died in a car accident when I was six."

Tiffany's eyes filled with pain and James reached over and rested his hand on Slade's shoulder. "We're so sorry."

The comforting touch overwhelmed him. "I didn't have an adoptive father. After that, I lived with her Aunt Liz until I turned eighteen. Liz passed away when I was in my first season of minor league ball."

"I'm so sorry you lost them both." Tiffany wiped away fresh tears. "All these years, I've worried, prayed, and hoped that you were okay, that you were in a loving home and had the best of everything."

The few memories he had about life with Jeannette were vague but happy. Letting them think he'd been surrounded by love at Liz's house was a kindness he could grant them. "I grew up on the beach and played a lot of baseball. Every kid's dream."

Tiffany smiled. "I'm glad. But I hate thinking that you've been all alone since Liz passed."

He thought of Liam, Dom, and Adam. Thanks to them, he hadn't been alone. "I have a great group of friends who've been there for me. I guess I created my own family."

"I've always carried you here." James brought a hand to his heart. "We want you to be a part of our family, as much or as little as you like."

"Yes, please," Tiffany added. "I'd love a chance to start over."

Fighting the urge not to tear up, he nodded. "I'd like that."

James stood. "Would you like to meet the rest of the crew?"

"Sure."

They led him into the kitchen where Liam sat with Melanie and a younger boy and girl. James stood behind the two, resting his hand on their shoulders. "This is Chloe and Caden. And…" He looked at Liam. "I'm sorry, but I don't know you."

Liam extended his hand. "I'm Liam. Slade's friend."

Melanie grinned at him. "I saw him waiting in the car and told him he could come in. I knew Mom wouldn't mind if we broke out the brownies. Here, Slade, have one."

Slade moved closer, needing the familiarity and solidity Liam provided in the midst of his muddled emotions and all the new faces.

Standing in the too-warm kitchen, they talked about baseball, and Tiffany and James' jobs, and his half-siblings' hobbies. The love between his parents and the loving relationship they shared with their kids was self-evident. Envy and longing twisted together like thorns on a vine. Slade didn't share history with any of them. The logical side of his brain knew he'd likely feel like an outsider for a while, but the emotional side wanted an immediate connection.

The surreal feeling he'd experienced with Melanie was back, and the enormity of the situation was almost too much to process. Overwhelmed and needing safe or neutral territory, he met Liam's gaze. "We should go."

The group walked them to the door and everyone made promises to keep in touch and get together again soon. Slade went through a round of hugs that felt both awkward and nice.

Too drained, he didn't even offer to drive. Simply slid into the passenger seat and dropped his head onto the headrest. While Liam laid a heavy foot onto the gas pedal, he stared out the window at the houses rolling by. Thoughts and emotions jumbled together, overlapping and conflicting until everything was a riot of confusion.

Liam didn't speak until they were in the elevator of their apartment building. "Dom and Adam are upstairs. They called when you were in with Tiffany and James. I figured you'd want them here."

Slade nodded. "Thanks."

His friends met them at the door. He accepted a beer from Adam and a hug from Dom. When they were settled into their usual places in the living room, Liam turned on the TV and searched until he landed on highlights from the evening's ballgames on the East Coast.

Dom nudged Slade's knee. "Well?"

"They're nice. I'm not sure what I feel or what's going to happen. I don't think we'll ever be as close as they are with their other kids. It's different, growing up with people compared to meeting them when you're a fully formed adult."

"The experiences you share going forward will help shape your relationship."

"I know." But it still wasn't the same. He took a long pull from the bottle. "I don't know that I'll ever look at them and think *Dad* and *Mom*, or call them that. It's too foreign a concept. Jeannette was my mom, and I don't even remember that much about her."

Beside him, Liam winced in sympathy and patted his arm.

Too many emotions rushed through him, lodging in his throat. He had to clear it before he could speak. "Growing up, the only thing I ever wanted was to be wanted. I never had that after Jeannette died."

Immediately, three heads swiveled in his direction. Liam's hand rested on Slade's left shoulder and Dom's landed on his right.

Liam spoke first. "Dude, I'm sorry. I hope we help make up for that a little. We always want you around."

Seated on the rug, Adam scooted closer. "You know we've got your back."

Dom's fingers dug in until Slade met his gaze. "Always. We're family."

Slade nodded. Swallowing a fresh lump in his throat, he smiled. "Thanks, guys."

He'd never felt loved. Not until he'd become friends with the trio surrounding him.

Dom had been the first person to ever say *I love you* to him. An *I love you, man* wrapped in smiles and back slaps and good feelings that had filled the empty space in his soul and soothed the ache of being alone.

Liam was his partner in crime. The other half of his brain. They just got each other. Same sense of humor, same taste in music, same ferocious loyalty to their friends and each other.

And Adam. The coolheaded reasoning, the one they could all count on to be logical.

The guys proved they had his back time and time again, always looking after him, always looking out for him, always wanting the best for him.

He'd been right in saying he'd created his own family. He just wasn't sure what to do about the one that had suddenly appeared, or how that puzzle piece would fit into the picture of his life.

CHAPTER THIRTEEN
CLAIRE

Claire walked into the office, desperate for coffee. The cup she'd downed on the way to the stadium hadn't helped clear the cobwebs of sleep at all. For the first time, she wished the ball game were already over. Too little sleep had left her off-balance. And grumpy.

A tie game and six extra innings the night before had meant entertaining the crowd until nearly midnight, and then she and Liam had joined Slade and Savanna, and Dom and Adam and their wives Irisa and Gemma for a drink. Getting to know everyone better had been a blast, but she was paying for it now.

Her sore muscles protested every movement and a dull headache brewed behind her eyes. Hopefully, this afternoon's game wouldn't drag on past nine. She made a bee-line for the single-cup coffee brewer next to the mini-fridge and chose a bold roast breakfast blend. Eye-opening caffeine with a hint of hazelnut.

The door opened and Liam swung through. Sans boot. But still using crutches.

Claire blinked and then looked at his leg again. Gray shorts, tanned calves, and sneakers.

Nope. Not seeing things. No boot.

He grinned. "Hey."

"Aren't you forgetting something?"

"Oh, right." He crossed to her slowly and placed a soft kiss on her lips.

She stifled a yawn. "That was nice but I meant, where's your boot?"

"Ditched it with Andy's approval this morning. I get to start physical therapy on Wednesday." He looked as excited as a kid with a pile of presents on Christmas morning.

"That's great. So, his two-week time frame was spot-on."

"The ankle still aches a lot and it's tight and still a little swollen, but he says that's normal. All systems go on recovery mode." He frowned. "No offense, but you look beat."

"I am beat. A frantic, six a.m. phone call from Lauren didn't help my beauty sleep."

"You're still beautiful."

"Thank you." Heat rushed into her cheeks.

"Is everything okay with your sister?"

"Yeah. Just teenage drama. It was fine by the time we ended the call."

"She's lucky to have you." He tossed his costume onto the couch. "After the game, why don't you come home with me? Slade won't be there, the team is flying to St. Louis right after the game. It'll be just you and me. We can have dinner. You can relax. I can hide your phone so your sisters don't bug you for a few hours."

Laughing, she leaned forward and kissed him. "That's the nicest offer I've had in a long time."

"Yeah? So if I add in a massage and drinks, does that increase the chances of you saying yes?"

She drained her coffee and set the cup aside, lifted by the anticipation of a laid-back Sunday evening with Liam. "I'm in."

Hours later, as early evening set in, she followed Liam into his apartment. She kicked off her flats, and stifling a yawn, walked right into his back. "Sorry."

"Careful, or I'll think you had more than one glass of wine with dinner." He turned and his eyes twinkled. "Want another?"

"Wine? I'll get it. You still can't carry things."

"Just for a few more days." He led her into the kitchen and nodded at the bottle of wine and two glasses on the counter. "I set these out this morning, hoping I'd be successful in convincing you to come over."

She smiled and worked on opening the bottle, then pouring the wine. "I'm glad you did. I needed tonight."

He moved to the freezer and pulled out an ice pack, then threw it on his shoulder to free his hands for the crutches. "We can sit in the living room."

Claire carried the glasses, admiring Liam's strong back and wide shoulders.

"Sit right here." He patted the middle couch cushion and then sat beside it and removed his sneakers. "I can massage your shoulders while I ice my ankle."

"Multitasking." She smiled and put the glasses down, then helped him elevate his foot and set the pack in place. The couch, a brown suede, had deep cushions that cradled the body.

His warm hands kneaded her shoulders, loosening the tight muscles. Her head lolled forward. "Feels so good."

"You're really tight."

"Mmm."

His fingers flexed on her neck, tiny circles of pleasure that slowly crept onto her scalp. Her hair tangled around his fingers but she didn't care. The sensation felt too good.

His other hand crept under her T-shirt, rubbing along her spine. She arched her back, stretching into him as his hand glided along her torso to rest on her stomach.

"Liam." She twisted toward him, seeking his mouth.

His teeth grazed her lips and he skimmed his fingers higher until they slid over the satin covering her breast.

She threaded her hands into his hair, holding onto him as the kiss deepened and his fingers explored. Goosebumps pebbled on her skin. She strained to get closer but her position prevented her from accessing more of him. Frustrated, she swung her leg over until she straddled him.

"There. That's better." Smiling, she stroked her fingers along his face.

His hands clamped at her waist. "Much better. Kiss me."

Leaning down, she licked her lips and watched his eyes darken. She flattened her hands on his shoulders, tilted her head, and brushed her lips over his, soft, light, and teasing.

He ran his hands up and down her back, and then under her shirt to follow the same path. Up, stopping at her bra clasp, working the clasp free, and then massaging with firm hands over every inch of skin.

Claire leaned back, desperate to see, to touch. She tugged his shirt over his torso. He stopped touching her long enough to yank the garment over his head and toss it across the room. Mouth gone dry, she gazed at his body. Tan skin stretched over developed muscles. He was a study in a well-built male. Her fingers itched to touch him. She traced the defined pecs. His skin was so warm under the sensitive pads of her fingers. When she reached his abs, he sucked in a breath and then groaned. His fingers tightened on her waist.

Eyes hot and wild, he inched her shirt up, his knuckles dragging along her skin. The shirt fell free and with a flick of his fingers, her bra straps slipped off her shoulders and it fell to her wrists. He gathered the material and twisted it until her hands were together, and then he lifted her arms high over her head so that her back arched and her breasts pressed into his chest. He worked his lips, teeth, and tongue over her jaw and neck, driving her crazy with nips on sensitive skin.

One hand drifted down and slid into the back pocket of her jeans. He cupped her rear and ground her into his erection.

Off balance, she could only lean into him. When he released his hold on her hands to slide his other hand to cup her rear, she tossed her bra aside and gripped his shoulders until he looked into her eyes. Panting, hard, and intense, he watched her as he continued to grind and she worked her hips into his.

Need spiraled through her as turbulent as a tornado.

They'd waited long enough. Had been pulled apart too many times with his injury and her family.

Tonight was for Liam. For her. For them.

"Do we need to move to the bedroom?"

"Probably. But you feel too good to move." He glided his hands up her back once again and then around to cup her breasts. After long moments, he dipped his head down and teased her with his lips, sending an arc of liquid desire directly to her core.

"Stand up."

The murmured request took a moment to register in her fuzzy brain. Buzzed on wine and Liam, she complied.

He traced his finger along her waistband, one slow,

continued caress across and back, and then he worked the button free. The zipper opened with one pull and he leaned forward, shifting on the cushion, and eased her jeans down her legs, leaving her in her underwear.

She stepped free of the pants and his hands fisted on his knees. "You're beautiful."

"And you're wearing too many clothes." She brushed his hand when he reached for her. "I'll help you."

Kneeling beside the couch, she trailed her fingers over his shorts, taking her time and making him groan. She leaned forward and pressed a kiss to his stomach, then kept her gaze on his as she slowly opened his shorts. His cloth covered arousal poked through the opening and she trailed her finger over it, relishing in Liam's deep groan.

His hand covered hers and he pulled her away. "Now, we need to move to the bedroom."

"Let me get your crutches."

"No. I don't want my arms holding onto them when I could be holding onto you. If you help me, I won't need them." He moved his leg off the ottoman and slowly stood up, and then shoved his shorts down to his feet and stepped free.

She stood by his left side. "Where do you want me?"

His eyes glittered. "That's a loaded question."

Fresh heat flushed through her body. "You know what I mean."

He wrapped his arm around her shoulder and drew her into his left side. She slid her arm around his waist. At times, she forgot their height difference was so great, but being skin on skin with him was a tantalizing reminder of his broad strength.

Walking down the hall, they stopped for kisses every few

steps. When they reached his bedroom doorway, he backed her against the threshold and kissed her breathless.

And then, he drew her inside.

Liam

After countless nights and fantasies, the real deal was here, and reality was so much better than fantasy.

Liam turned on the lamp by the bedside table, but left the rest of the room cast in darkness. Reaching for Claire, he moved carefully as his eyes adjusted. She was a goddess. Hair like gold, eyes like aquamarine, and her small body, delicate yet strong. Not only physical strength, but emotional too.

She was a giver, over and over again. She needed someone to make sure she was taken care of too, and he nominated himself for the job.

Claire linked their fingers together and stepped into him. Holding hands at the foot of his bed, they kissed. Slow and sexy, the moment seared into Liam's memory.

This woman.

He was over his head for her.

He grazed his fingers up the silky skin of her arms. Hers followed the same path on his. When he reached her shoulders, he continued the journey down the sides of her torso, causing her to shiver, and then teased over the blue striped underwear that rode low on her hip. Needing more, he sat on the bed and pulled her between his legs.

She stroked her hands over his chest, driving him crazy. "Is your ankle hurting?"

He had no idea. His head was too clouded with lust and

the beautiful, almost naked woman in his arms. "Something else is."

Claire's fingers traced over his thighs, over his boxers, stroking his length. He rested his forehead against hers and edged his fingers under her panties, determined to drive her as high as she drove him, working his fingers against her until she clutched at his shoulders and gasped his name. Then he did it again.

When they were both panting and straining together for *more*, he pulled her onto the bed and rolled until he covered her with his body. Caging her with his hands on both sides of her head, he leaned down and kissed her, then he worked his boxers down and kicked free. Claire arched her body and shimmied out of her underwear. It sailed past his head on its way to the floor.

Grinning at her, he lay on his side, facing her, and drew her against him. They rocked together, their fingers seeking to draw out pleasure, guided by whispered requests and gasps and groans.

Liam rolled away and dug through the bedside table drawer until he found a condom. Protection in place, he moved between her legs. He braced one hand by her shoulder and together, they guided him to her center.

Throbbing with overwhelming need, he paused, drinking in her lips swollen from his kisses and her eyes misted in passion. Smiling, Claire curled her other hand around his neck. "Kiss me."

He complied, tangling their tongue together. Her legs encircled his waist and then her heels dug in, urging him on. He sunk inside in one slow, smooth slide. His eyes closed and he groaned as her tight, wet heat gripped him.

Claire's fingers in his hair held him close and they came together in breathless thrusts. He wasn't going to last long this first time. She felt too good. Perfect, actually. But damn, he was determined that she hit her peak first. He hitched her leg higher and rolled his hips—faster, deeper, harder. Until he was steeped in her feel, scent, and taste and still, it wasn't enough.

Those fingers tightened in warning as her release hit and she shuddered around him.

Liam pressed his lips to hers, drinking in her gasps. Pleasure tingled at the base of his spine. He bucked his hips wildly until his release crashed over him like a tidal wave.

He collapsed, boneless. When he had the strength to move, he shifted to his side, dealt with the condom, and then drew her against him.

She smiled and kissed him, snuggling into him with a sigh. Her fingers traced patterns over his chest that both relaxed and teased.

His brain was fried. He couldn't think of a single thing to say.

He combed his fingers through her hair, amazed that he finally had her in his bed.

She looked good there.

Damn good.

He wanted her all over again.

But her breathing had slowed and deepened and the hand tracing over his skin grew heavy and then stopped. Eyes closed, her body relaxed fully as she fell to sleep.

Liam dragged the blanket at the foot of the bed up with his foot. Shifting carefully so he wouldn't disturb his sleeping beauty, he pulled the blanket over them, then switched off the light.

He lay in the darkness with his arm wrapped around Claire's waist, mulling over the effects of fate.

Maybe the busted ankle had happened so that they'd come

into each other's lives. His mother always said that the best things came along when you weren't looking for them. He hadn't been looking for Claire, but he couldn't deny the spark he'd immediately felt upon meeting her, or how it had grown stronger and brighter until it could power all of LA.

He'd tried to push aside the thoughts about what would happen or could happen after he'd been cleared to return to his job, but they continued to creep in, especially now that he was about to begin physical therapy. The uncertainty was too great. What he needed to do was enjoy the next several weeks with Claire, definitely doing a lot more of what they'd done tonight, but the little things too.

She sighed in her sleep and shifted closer. Liam pressed a kiss to her forehead and wrapped his arm tighter around her. He liked having her close. The old line *keep your friends close and your enemies* closer flitted through his mind. Claire wasn't his enemy, even though she might end up with his job if things didn't go well. She definitely was his friend, but more than that, too.

He thought of Fin and Fiona. Fin had found his mate, even though Great Whites were mostly solitary creatures. Liam hadn't ever given the matter much thought, too wrapped up in his job and his friends to think about his future or who he wanted to share it with.

But Claire made him think.

CHAPTER FOURTEEN

SLADE

Slade stood and stretched and then gathered his bag from the bus's overhead compartment. One week on the road, four games in St. Louis, followed by three games in Milwaukee, followed by the slowest flight and bus ride of his life, and finally, they'd arrived back at the baseball stadium's parking lot.

Most of his teammates were talking about getting into their cars and going home to their families or significant others. A few others were planning to hit the closest bar.

He should go home and rest his body, but eight o'clock on a Sunday evening wasn't too late to stop in and see Savanna.

Dom waited for him outside the bus. "Heading home?"

"Nah. I thought I might take a drive."

"Any place in particular? Like Savanna's."

"Yeah. Like Savanna's."

"Let me give you some advice." Dom patted the roof of his car. "Go for it. But make it last." He grinned, his pearly whites practically glowing in the dark. "See you here tomorrow."

Slade nodded and hugged him and then headed to his car.

He hadn't been sure what time the game would end or how the flight or bus ride would be, so he hadn't called her in case their arrival would be delayed.

Hopefully, she wouldn't mind him showing up, unannounced.

Thirty minutes later, he knocked on her door.

Locks clicked, and then it opened. Savanna's hair was drawn into a high ponytail and she wore a white tank top and gray shorts that rode high on her hips. Smiling, she launched herself into Slade's arms. Slade slung his travel bag behind him as he adjusted his grip around Savanna's waist. He pressed his hand into the small of her back and walked her the few steps inside. His mouth fused to hers as he kicked the door closed behind him.

Need. The word pounded through him with every beat of his heart.

So much need.

He set her down to lock the door and drop his bag on the floor. And then he cradled her face in his hands. "Hi."

"Hi." Her hands traveled up his chest and curled into his shirt. Like a magnet seeking its mate, she strained toward him.

Stroking his thumb against her cheek, he lowered his head until their lips met.

They'd seen each other once more the weekend after their para-sailing adventure and his visit with his parents, for a quick drink last Saturday night. He and Savanna had spent time with Liam and Claire, Dom and his wife Irisa, and Adam and his wife Gemma before the guys had left for the road trip. He'd loved how the eight of them had gotten along. But right now, last Saturday seemed pretty far away.

Her hands clung to his biceps and she angled her head seeking a deeper taste. Slade was glad to accommodate. His tongue tangled with hers, firm licks that stoked his need higher when she caressed his with equal passion. He moved his hands over her, desperate to touch every inch. Slade traced the line of her neck, the slope of her shoulder, and across her collarbones. She wasn't wearing a bra. That thought registered a second before he grazed his fingers along her nipples straining against the shirt's material.

Soft fingers worked at the buttons of his shirt, opening the row quickly from the top down. Savanna kissed him as she freed the buttons. He hardened at the thought of her hands on his skin.

Savanna pulled his shirt free of his pants and pushed it off his shoulders. He pulled his T-shirt over his head and dropped it beside them. The only thing he hated about team travel was that they had to wear suits. But watching her help take his off… yeah, he could get used to that.

Savanna's eyes widened and her hands mapped the muscles in his chest and torso. Her touch almost burned into his sensitive skin. He needed to feel more of her skin against his.

Lifting the edge of her tank, he slipped the material off, baring her to him. Curves and softness and beauty, her body was perfect. He filled his hands with her breasts. Her eyes closed and she bit her lip. Slade trailed kisses along her neck.

His control slipped when her fingers opened his belt. Eyes on his, she worked open the button and zipper on his pants. With unsteady hands, he moved to return the favor, but his hand met only soft cotton. Blinking through the haze, he looked down at the material.

She smiled. "These are easy. There's a drawstring inside the waistband."

He delved his fingers between her stomach and the shorts, found the string, and pulled it loose. Easing the shorts down her legs, he discovered she wore no underwear. A bolt of lust hit him, but before he could explore further, she slid his pants and boxers down in one smooth move and then sank to her knees.

Slade went rock hard as Savanna took him in her hands, and then into her mouth. Wet heat enveloped him. He rested his fingers in her hair, not pushing, but needing to touch her. He mentally recited the league standings to keep himself under control. When he nearly lost the edge, he eased her back and to her feet, and then crushed his mouth to hers.

"My turn." Stepping free of his pants and shoes, he hitched her off her feet, urging her to wrap her legs around his waist. Intending to walk to the bedroom, he decided the couch was far enough, and kicked his pants in that direction so the condom in his pocket would be close by. He shifted one hand to her hip and laid her body on the couch, then moved between her thighs.

He sat back, stroking a path up her legs, watching for any hint of a sensitive area that he could explore later. Savanna's hands closed over his and she guided him to her center. He leaned forward and slipped his fingers into her, growing harder at the catch of her breath. Wanting to drench her in pleasure, he followed the path with his mouth. She arched toward him with a moan at the dual assault and threaded her fingers into his hair as she continued to move her hips in time to his movements.

He pulled away to retrieve the condom and rejoined her with a kiss. He couldn't get enough of kissing her.

Savanna took the condom and with smooth strokes, rolled it on him.

Keeping their gazes connected, he lifted her hips and filled her. Twin gasps echoed in the room. He paused for a moment, throbbing inside her, waiting for her to get used to him.

They fit together like they were made for one another. Lined up just right. He slowly pulled back and then thrust again. Leaning on his forearms, he brought their lips together as he increased the pace with snapping hips and she met him move for move.

Fast approaching the edge, he slipped one hand between them, stroking Savanna in time with his thrusts. That touch was enough to send her over, and with pleasure spiking his blood and spiraling through his system, he followed right behind.

Being with her settled something inside him and filled part of the space that had stubbornly remained empty his entire life. Trusting that she would stay, that he wouldn't be left alone, was so hard, but he wanted to believe it. She clung to him like she had no intention of letting him go.

He knew he should get up, move, deal with the condom, but he didn't have the energy to do more than shift their bodies until she lay half on top of him. She smiled at him and linked their hands together and then brought them up to rest over his heart.

He'd fallen for her fast, hard, and completely. Spiraled past lust and infatuation and straight into love. But until he had a better idea of how she felt, he couldn't tell her.

CHAPTER FIFTEEN

CLAIRE

Stupid flat tire.

Stupid special-sized tire that couldn't be delivered until the next day.

Phone in hand, Claire paced the mechanic's small waiting area and sighed. The room smelled of stale coffee and motor oil.

Things could be worse. At least her phone was fully charged and she wasn't stranded on the side of a deserted road in the dead of night.

But she was totally bummed. She'd been looking forward to spending the day with Savanna for more than a week, but was going to miss out on relaxing facials, massages and pedicures at the spa with her new friend. All because someone didn't have the good sense to keep an eye on their dog. Thank goodness she'd swerved and missed the sweet little puppy. Of course, she'd clipped a curb at fifty miles an hour, damaging her tire and bending the rim beyond repair.

She couldn't blame the dog. The only silver lining so far was that the mechanic had been close by.

But he didn't have a loaner car for her to use.

She needed a ride, but so far, none of her sisters had returned her call. Calling a rental shop seemed more trouble that it was worth, with the mechanic's promise that he'd drive her car to wherever she wanted as soon as it was ready.

She dialed Savanna, but the call went to voice mail. She was probably on her way to the spa. Hopefully, she'd get the message before she drove too far.

Whenever her sisters had car trouble, they called her. Like they expected her to know why their cars weren't working. Like they expected her to drop everything and rush over to wait with them until the auto club or a tow truck arrived, which she always did if they were stuck somewhere alone.

Whenever they needed anything, she was their first call. She didn't mind doing things for them, but at times, she wished they'd take some personal responsibility. After all, she had been younger than Lauren when all the parental duties had fallen onto her shoulders. She wished for someone *she* could lean on, too.

Liam's face filled her mind. He would do anything for his friends. She liked to think they were growing close enough where she could count on him if she needed to. She already knew she'd do anything for him.

She dialed his number. He was probably in the middle of his physical therapy appointment, but maybe he could pick her up after he'd finished.

The call went to voice mail. She smiled at his voice and the recording and kept her voice light, breezy, and free of the disappointment weighing down her stomach. "Hey, I need a ride. I'm stuck at an auto shop near the coffee place we went to last weekend. My car got a flat and won't be ready until sometime tomorrow."

Fifteen minutes later, just as she'd resigned herself to

calling a cab, her phone pinged with a text. Hoping for Liam or one of her sisters, she was surprised by Savanna's name.

Savanna: Hey, are you still waiting at the auto shop?

Claire: Yep. Sorry I had to cancel on you.

Savanna: No worries. The spa will let us reschedule our appointments. Send me the address. I'll pick you up.

Surprise and gratitude filled her. Claire sent the address and a series of happy face emojis.

When Savanna arrived, she waved off Claire's thanks and insisted on stopping to treat Claire to coffee, an iced concoction drizzled with chocolate in a colorful coffee cup print that they sipped at an outside table under a large white umbrella.

Savanna gestured at her car. "Five years ago, I was on my way home from a fundraiser and my engine seized. I was without my car for over a week. One of the guys I used to work with had lived sort of near me and gave me a ride to and from the office. I gave him money for gas and bought him lunch all that week. When I got my car back, he sent me an email, like a bill if you can believe it, charging me for the wear and tear of having an extra person in his car. I was shocked. Any time after that, I either rented a car or borrowed my parents' spare. At least they don't charge crazy, made-up fees."

Claire rolled her eyes. "What an ass. That's too awful. But I'll give you gas money."

Savanna shot her a narrowed glance over her cup. "No. That is *not* the reason I told you the story. The point was that it's nice to have someone there when you need it, even if they are a little anal about their cars. My parents drive me crazy a lot, but it is nice knowing that no matter what, they'll always be there."

"I didn't really have that. My dad always worked a lot. He would help with something if he could, and if I needed something, he'd make sure I got it, but I had to figure a lot of things out on my own. And then my sisters turned to me. I can't believe none of them called me back today. They're all home on summer vacation." The muscles around her heart tugged. She hadn't realized how much their lack of concern bothered her until she'd said it. She shrugged and smiled. "I'm glad you came."

Savanna tapped her cup against Claire's. "Of course. What are friends for?"

Liam

Physical therapy wasn't easy, then again, Liam hadn't expected it to be. But he hadn't counted on how much things would hurt. He'd been working hard, sessions three times a week for the past two weeks, in addition to doing the exercises three times a day at home, and was beginning to see some progress along with the diminished aches and swelling.

After ninety minutes of stretching and strength-building exercises, followed by time on the treadmill, he sighed in relief at his ten minutes with an ice pack.

Usually, he worked out alone with the physical therapist in one of the stadium's training rooms. But today, Dom, Slade, and Adam occupied the room with him. Dom and Adam were getting in some preventative care with one of the trainers and Slade had tagged along because they were going to lunch afterward. Having his buddies around him made everything easier.

Slade sat in a chair near the training table, playing with his phone. "Hey, Li, I found a new ring tone to use just for you. Call me so you can hear it."

Liam felt the pocket of his shorts. "I left my phone in the car. Play it from yours."

Slade held up his phone and menacing cello music filled the room.

Liam burst out laughing. "Dude, really? The theme for *Jaws*?"

"Funny, right?" Slade looked proud of himself.

"It's great."

It *was* great. He was on his way to fully regaining his job as Fin, attacking his recovery the way a shark attacked its prey.

He left PT sore but energized and rode with Slade to the restaurant, a cafe they frequented with a discrete wait staff and a large selection of beer.

He waited until they were served and then looked at Adam and Dom. "Since PT is going so well, I think I'll be close to one hundred percent by the All-Star game. I can probably go back to watching your dogs during road trips then too. I miss the fur balls."

Dom laughed. "I think a full grown Aikita and Great Dane are a little large to be called fur balls. It would be great to get things back to normal though. Irisa has been busy with the band working on a new record. I know she'll appreciate it when you can help out again."

Adam picked up his glass. "You're one of the few people Bear trusts when Gemma and I aren't around. Having you back would help out a lot. I hope it works out by then."

"Cool." Feeling more settled, Liam dug into his food. Watching his friends' dogs had started a few years earlier when the guys needed someone they trusted who would be home in L.A. during the team's road trips. He loved those dogs. They helped fill the hours when his friends were away.

Slade raised his brow. "Does Claire even like dogs?"

Liam paused with his fork halfway to his mouth. "I don't know."

He'd never even thought about it, but considering he had the dogs with him for essentially half of baseball season, he'd better find out. If their relationship continued the way it had been, they'd be spending a lot of days and nights together. She would probably have an opinion about two dogs that each weighed over one hundred pounds wanting to sleep in their bed. "I'll text her now. What time were she and Savanna supposed to be finished at the spa?"

Slade shrugged. "Beats me. She said she'd text me after they'd finished."

He patted his pocket and swore. "Damn phone is still in the car."

Adam turned to Slade. "Speaking of Savanna, you seem more settled lately. Is she why?"

Slade spent a minute poking his food with his fork. "She matters. A lot. But I don't know what I'm doing there. Feels like I'm at the plate, with a full count, bottom of the ninth, bases loaded, and my next swing has the potential to win us the championship or lose us our chance."

Liam exchanged glances with Adam and Dom. He didn't have any advice to offer his best friend. He wasn't an expert on relationships.

Dom patted Slade's shoulder. "But you're a pro at remaining cool and patient up there, even when working on a full count or fouling off ten in a row."

Adam nodded in agreement, but Liam frowned. "What the hell does that even mean?"

"That he won't be able to predict what's thrown at him, so he needs to relax and enjoy the relationship, not freeze up and over-think his every move."

Liam was impressed. "You're pretty smart about this relationship stuff."

Dom chuckled. "I don't know if I'd go that far. But I do know that if you're always focused on what's coming next, you miss a lot of great moments along the way."

When they returned to Slade's car, Liam hopped in the passenger seat and grabbed his phone from the console.

Missed call: Claire. Three hours ago.

Slade slid his phone it the space Liam's had vacated. "Savanna just sent a text. She's at Claire's apartment."

"Oh, they're back from the spa already?"

"They didn't go. Seems Claire had car trouble on the way."

Frowning and concerned, he listened to Claire's message about being stuck and needing a ride. Her voice and tone were flatter and thinner, like she was upset but pretending hard not to be. He hated not having been there when she'd needed him. "We should go over and see them."

He made Slade stop so he could get flowers and wine. Half an hour later, they knocked on Claire's door. As soon as she opened it, he shoved his gifts at his friend and pulled Claire into his arms. "I'm sorry I wasn't there when you needed me."

"It's okay." Her voice was muffled by his shirt. "I managed. And Savanna came to my rescue."

"Still." He brushed his hand over her hair and continued to hold her against his chest. "What happened?"

"A dog ran into the road and I swerved to avoid it. Messed up my tire and rim pretty bad. I don't even care about the car. I'm just so glad I didn't hit the dog."

He leaned back enough to stroke her face. "You like dogs?"

"Love them. But I could never have one growing up because two of my sisters are allergic."

He grinned. He couldn't wait to introduce her to Champ and Bear. "You could get your own now."

Or, they could get one together.

The immediate suggestion popped into his mind and stopped his hand mid-caress. Buying a pet together was something people did after moving in together. He was jumping ahead, too far and too fast.

"I've been thinking about it." Claire unwound from his hold and stepped back. Hitching her head to the side, she motioned for them to come inside. "I can't decide if I want something huge or something tiny."

"We'd have to make sure it plays well with Champ and Bear." Still struck by the *let's buy a puppy together* thought, he followed her into her living room. "They're really friendly though. Good dogs."

"Who are they and why do they need to get along with my future pet?"

"When Dom and Adam go on road trips, they leave their dogs with me." He tugged his phone from his pocket and thumbed through photos until he landed on one of the dogs.

Her eyes widened, and then a smile curved her lips. "They're massive."

"They still think they're lap dogs." He tapped another photo of him on the couch, buried under the pair. "See?"

"Aww." Chuckling, she leaned against his side. "But I've been to your place when the team has been away. Where were you hiding the dogs? Your place is big, but I'm pretty sure I would've seen or heard them."

"Believe me, you wouldn't be able to miss them. I haven't been mobile enough to keep them since I've been laid up with the broken ankle. But since recovery is going well, I should be able to watch them during the first road trip after the All-Star game."

"I can't wait to meet them."

Liam pocketed his phone. He'd have to be careful. They could be overzealous in their greeting, and he wouldn't risk Claire getting hurt for anything.

"Liam," Slade called from the kitchen. "I'm opening the wine."

He'd been so caught up in Claire, he'd forgotten Slade and Savanna were even there. Laughing, he slid his arm around Claire's shoulder and walked with her into the kitchen, determined to do everything he could to make sure she had a good night.

Dom's earlier words echoed in his head. *If you're always focused on what's coming next, you miss a lot of great moments along the way.* He didn't want to miss a single moment with Claire, but the further she became intertwined in his life, he couldn't help wondering what would happen next, or how they would be affected when he fully resumed his mascot duties.

CHAPTER SIXTEEN
SLADE

He was having the worst game of his season, maybe his career.

From his position at first base, Slade surveyed the scoreboard and wished they were already at the bottom of the ninth instead of the top. He'd gone zero-for-three in his at-bats, had committed a costly error in the second inning that resulted in Colorado taking the lead, and already had a huge welt forming on his ribs from a collision with the dugout railing while trying to catch a pop-up foul ball that he thought he should have caught.

A Sunday afternoon ball game in late June, with the sky a cloudless blue and a soft breeze blowing across the field should have been fun. Except they were losing their tenth game in a row. The fans weren't happy. His teammates weren't happy. The GM wasn't happy. And Dusty definitely wasn't happy.

Slade's gaze drifted toward the stands. His birth parents and half-siblings were sitting on the first base side, right behind the dugout. He'd thought of nothing else since they'd called to say they'd gotten tickets and were excited to see him play. They were supposed to meet up with him after the game too.

He saw them every time he walked back to the dugout, and he truly understood why some of the guys had a hard time playing in front of their families or old coaches. The emotion of playing in front of them combined with the mounting pressure to be the best and play a perfect game often worked against a player.

His concentration pinged from Tiffany, James, and crew to Savanna, sitting with Dom and Adam's wives, and finally back to the field.

Top of the ninth inning. Still a one-run game. Bases loaded, one out. The batter hit a sharp ground ball to first. Slade quickly got in front of it and knocked the ball down with his body and then picked it up bare-handed and rushed to throw to home plate, too high for Mario to catch. It flew behind the catcher who clearly wasn't expecting the ball.

As soon as he released the ball, Slade shook his head at his actions, and his momentary lapse of sense. He should have tried to turn a routine double play to end the inning, not throw to home. That was a mistake a player made in the minors, not the pros. Overthrowing the catcher was another mark against him, allowing two runs to score on his errant throw.

Shit.

The Riptide were down by three runs, and they were all his fault.

Thankfully, the pitcher struck out the next two batters to end the inning. But the damage was already done.

He apologized to his teammates as they walked to the dugout and most of the guys waved him off and told him not to worry about it. But Dusty's glare could have burned holes through Slade's body.

"Goddamn it, MacInnes!" Dusty stopped him at the bottom of the steps. "What the hell is wrong with you today? You're playing like shit. Get your head out of your ass and back on the field."

Slade nodded and walked past, ignoring the tirade as the manager continued to bellow. He sat hard on the bench with his head in his hands.

Dom sat beside him and tapped his shoulder. "You okay?"

"It's hard to focus."

"I can imagine. Hang in there. We just need to get a couple guys on base."

His teammates helped bail him out by scoring two quick runs to bring the Riptide back within one again. The rally carried on long enough to get Slade back to the plate. One last chance to redeem himself with two outs and guys on second and third. All he had to do was get the ball out of the infield and he had a good chance of knocking in two runs to win the game. But before he knew it, he was down zero-for-two in the count after fouling off the first two pitches. He knew he was in trouble because the pitcher now had a clear advantage over him, and could throw his best stuff at Slade.

And he did.

Slade adjusted his helmet one last time before glaring at the pitcher. He got into his batting stance. The crowd went wild, on its feet, cheering this last chance.

The pitcher threw a hard curve ball that started at Slade's shoulders and quickly dropped into the strike zone, fooling Slade completely, and leaving him standing with his bat in his hands as the umpire called him out. Strike three. Striking out without swinging the bat was the worst possible way to end the game.

The crowd went silent.

Slade stayed in the batter's box, head down, while the catcher moved past him to congratulate the pitcher.

All the excitement drained from the stadium, the fans headed to the exits.

This was now officially the worst game of his career.

He walked to the dugout, not looking at the stands. Most of his teammates had cleared out but Dom and Adam waited there.

With Dusty.

His manager met him at the top of the dugout. "What the hell were you looking at out there?"

Slade dropped his bat. "I fucked up. He fooled me. What do you want me to say? It was a good pitch."

"I should have benched your ass after your last fuck up. Your head hasn't been in the game at all. You're done. Benched. I'll give Russo a chance at first base for the rest of the week."

"What the fuck?" Slade slammed his helmet on the ground. Anger boiled in his veins. He stepped closer, hands clenched into fists at his sides. "You can't do that."

"I can do whatever the fuck I want." Dusty jammed his finger into Slade's chest, pushing hard with every word. "Keep talking. You'll be riding the bench for longer."

"Get your hands off me, asshole."

"Asshole?" Dusty's eyes narrowed and he shoved Slade back a step. "You're done for the season."

"Push me again, old man, and I'll knock your wrinkly ass out."

Dom, Adam, and the third base coach rushed over. Pulling Slade back, Dom got in between Dusty and him. He nudged Slade, directing him down the dugout steps. "Calm down. Let's go. That's enough."

Slade glared at the field where the third base coach was trying to calm Dusty down. "Did you hear what he said? That prick's trying to bench me."

Adam joined them and patted him on the back. "Let's get to the showers. You need to cool off."

"Yeah." He headed for the showers, intent on avoiding any conversations and just getting the hell out of the ballpark.

When he left the locker room, Tim from security met him in the hall. After a quick glance around, Tim pulled him to the side. "The GM called Dusty up to his office. Rumor has it that he's being let go. No official word yet though."

"Whoa. That would make my night. Thanks for the heads-up."

Word had spread fast. The halls buzzed with gossip. Proving once again that they had his back, Dom and Adam entertained the reporters long enough for Slade to slip out.

He tried to put the game and speculation over Dusty out of his mind while he drove to the bar. It was one of a one-hundred-sixty-two game season. They had another game tomorrow. Dwelling on this one wouldn't help. But damn it, did he have to screw up so badly? No way would he let the old man bench him.

Parking next to Savanna's car, he realized she was still sitting in the driver's seat. Seeing him, she jumped out and shut the door. She crossed to him, her red sundress showing off curves he'd touched only hours before.

When her arms wound around his neck and her lips pressed to his, the tension melted from his muscles. He wrapped his arms around her and soaked in the serenity she gave him.

After a long moment, she eased back. "Are you all right?"

"Better now." He kissed her cheek and hugged her closer, and then drew away.

"Tiffany and James are meeting us inside?"

"They're probably already here." He held the door for her and kept one arm around her as they wove through the room toward his birth parents and half-siblings. Crowded around a booth, the group waved.

James stood when they arrived. "Exciting game this afternoon."

"Not one of my best." Slade managed the smile more easily, but his embarrassment and irritation at his actions on the field still stung.

"Every player has a bad game now and again." James patted him on the shoulder. "You're a top contender with the fans' vote for the All-Star team, so just put it out of your mind and worry about the next game."

Slade made the introductions between Savanna and the others, and then they slid into the booth beside Tiffany.

She patted his hand. "I didn't like the way the manager got in your face when you were in the dugout. He shouldn't be allowed to talk to you guys that way."

"For him, that was pretty mild. But yeah, I agree. A personality like Dusty's can become a cancer in the clubhouse." It already had. Most of his teammates were grumbling about Dusty and the tension in the clubhouse was thicker than he'd ever experienced. Who knew what would come of Dusty's conversation with the GM?

Under the table, Savanna's hand squeezed his thigh. "I wanted to run down there and tell him to back off. I saw what happened after the game. He's awful."

He covered her hand with his, pleased at her protectiveness. "Thanks."

His phone buzzed with texts from Dom, Adam, and Liam.

Dom: Time to celebrate. Dusty is officially fired.

Adam: GM is holding a press conference now. Said what happened after the game was the last straw and it was clear Dusty had lost the locker room.

Liam: Dude! Celebration tonight!

The weight hovering over his heart lightened and he couldn't contain the grin spreading over his face. "I just got word that Dusty's gone. Fired tonight."

"Good riddance to him." James nodded and then smiled. "I never liked him as a manager. And I especially disliked his treatment of you. Let's celebrate."

Slade wrapped his arm around Savanna's shoulders and turned his attention to the people around the table. Celebrating worked for him.

They sat for more than an hour, over shared appetizers and a mix of drinks, and he got to know the family a little better.

He definitely was less of a stranger to his family than before. But he still felt like an outsider.

Savanna

After his bio family left, Savanna and Slade moved to the bar. She'd been pleased when he'd asked her to go with him to meet them. Curiosity over who they were and the knowledge that Slade needed her had made for an easy yes. "I liked them."

"I do too. I'm hoping that they'll eventually feel more like friends than strangers. Even family."

She squeezed his thigh in reassurance. "I'm sure they will."

Slade wrapped his arm around her shoulder as the bartender set fresh drinks on the table. "I was thinking about vacations for the off-season, and there's something I wanted to ask you."

He was including her in his months-away plans. Heat and pleasure curled through her system. "Ask away."

"How do you feel about swimming with sharks?"

She blinked, surprised at the unexpected question. "You're serious?"

"Yeah. There's a five-day trip, cage diving off the coast of Mexico's Guadalupe Island. We're guaranteed to see sharks. Up close. What do you say?" Eyes shining, he lifted his brows. "Five days on the water. You and me."

"That part sounds good, but the shark part?" Voluntarily getting up close and personal with one of the ocean's deadliest predators seemed crazy. She'd have a hard enough time dealing with the flight to Mexico.

The bartender sidled over toward them. Blonde and busty, she leaned over to scoop up the empty glasses. Unashamed of eavesdropping or flashing her cleavage, she shot Slade a slow smile of obvious invitation. "I'd do it in a minute."

Irritation, unease, and jealousy twisted together, and Savanna kept her arm below the bar to avoid hauling off and punching the woman for infringing on their conversation and on her man. What was she supposed to say—that instead of scary sharks, she'd prefer swimming with happy dolphins at a luxury resort? Yeah, right. That sounded really brave. Ignoring the woman, she twisted toward Slade, pleased when the hand draped over her shoulder pulled her closer.

Slade shot the blonde a semblance of a smile and immediately turned to Savanna. He linked their fingers together under the table. "They follow a careful safety protocol. You remember what I told you. I do a lot of research and I'll always keep you safe. When we get home, I'll show you the website."

When we get home… They spent most nights together now, enough to keep clothes and toiletries at each other's places.

He moved their linked hands to rest on the bar, in plain sight of the bartender and anyone else interested. "I've never done this before and I think it would be something really cool to share together."

She loved that he wanted to share experiences with her. But some of his ideas were dangerous, especially to someone like her. Even so, she squared her shoulders and lifted her chin, projecting as much confidence as she could manage. "I'd love to see the site."

Grinning, he talked about the accommodations and amenities and how they should take an intro to diving course together to prepare. Like this trip was a definite, and her confidence was acceptance of the plan.

With the bartender hovering, Savanna couldn't relax or talk to Slade about limitations. Catching the blonde's eye, she frosted her voice. "Can we have the check?"

Slade slid his hand down Savanna's back and nuzzled her neck. "Good call. Let's get out of here. My apartment is closer, so let's spend the night there."

The blonde came back. With a smirk at Savanna, she pushed a glass with the check rolled inside to Slade. A piece of paper behind it had her name and number scrawled across the bottom.

He glanced at the check and stuffed it back in the cup with some bills, burying the offending piece of paper. Savanna smirked in return at his action and slid her hand into his back pocket as they exited the bar.

Once they were tucked into his bed with his laptop,

looking at the shark dive site, she broached the subject. "When we were para-sailing, I mentioned that I didn't think I ever wanted to go skydiving, and you said that was okay."

"It is. I'll never force you to do something you don't want to do."

"I don't think I ever want to do bungee jumping either. Or hang-gliding. Or cliff diving. And when I ski, I stick to the bunny trail."

His brows knit in confusion. "Okay?"

"I like that we've taken some risks. But I still have fears, and I think some might be self-preserving."

"I know. We still need to get you back to that diving board and the firehouse pole." He cupped her face with his hand. "If the sharks are too much, you don't have to go. I'll never push you past your limits."

You don't have to go, not *we won't go*.

If she stayed, he'd still take that vacation. Maybe with someone else. Someone like that blonde bartender. She didn't like that at all. But she also didn't want to feel like she had to do things she didn't want to do just to hang onto him. "I'll think about the sharks. The cages are really strong. And seeing them up close would be amazing."

He grinned and then drew her close. His lips closed over hers, firm and warm. Too soon, he pulled back. "We can do anything you want too. Just name it, and I'll make it happen."

His enthusiasm and generosity were overwhelming. But he operated from a base of no fear. Making promises like that were easy to him. No risk on his part because he was brave enough to take on the world.

She wanted to be with him and he wanted to be with her, but was that enough when they were so different in their tastes? She'd known a couple who'd divorced after twenty years of marriage because their differences outweighed their similarities.

She didn't want Slade to grow to resent her for not wanting to try things that he wanted them to share. But she also didn't want to be forced past a reasonable comfort zone either.

Maybe they were too different to be together.

CHAPTER SEVENTEEN

LIAM

Liam increased his pace to a faster walk on the treadmill and settled his attention on the TV hanging on the wall. His ankle felt pretty good. One week to go until the All-Star game. He wasn't back to jumps yet, but Andy had approved a few small, easy stunts. He couldn't wait to race across the field on the ATV and hear the fans cheer.

Fin's comeback was so close, he could almost taste it.

On screen, highlights of the previous day's Riptide game played. He cheered when they showed Slade's grand slam home run. The team's abrupt firing of Dusty had flipped a switch for the team. All the guys were playing better because they loved and respected the new manager, a former player who had mentored Dom in his rookie days.

Happy for his buddies, he watched the ball fly though the air and pumped his fist in celebration.

His stomach clutched as his feet flew out behind him and he scrambled to stop his fall.

Too late.

Landing on the floor, he rolled his healing ankle. White

spots dotted his vision. Gasping and wincing and cursing at the pain, he collapsed, grabbing at his ankle.

Andy and the personal trainer rushed over, checking him, asking questions. Liam rubbed his hands over his face. This wasn't good.

After an x-ray and a thorough examination, he sat on the training table, staring at his ankle in disbelief.

The mild sprain was better than a major one, but it was still enough to throw a wrench into his recovery.

And ruin his plans for the All-Star game.

Fuck.

Andy rolled the elastic bandage around Liam's foot and ankle. "You need to keep weight off of your foot for three days. Elevate the injured or sore area on pillows while applying ice and anytime you are sitting or lying down. Apply the ice or cold pack for ten to twenty minutes, three or more times a day. After forty-eight to seventy-two hours, if swelling is gone, apply heat to the area that hurts. If by Thursday, you feel like you still need the support of the bandage, call me." He paused and met Liam's gaze. "Scratch that. I want to see you in here on Thursday and look at it myself."

"Don't trust me to be honest, Doc?"

"I know how upset you are about being relegated to the golf cart for the big game. So no, not right now. Even though you didn't feel pain in your ankle before the sprain happened, it was still swollen from the prior injury, and now, from the sprain, it's swollen even more and there's pain."

"Okay. I'll try to stop in." Nope. Not gonna happen. He'd manage on his own.

"There's a game Thursday night, so if you don't come to me during the day, I'll easily be able to track you down when you're in Fin's costume."

He heaved a sigh. "Fine."

"I know you're disappointed. You were progressing well. My hope was that you'd be ready to return to the field with at least some of your gymnastics moves by the end of July. I can't promise that now. The plyometric exercises will have to be pushed off for at least a few more weeks, and we'll need to take them slowly. I know you're not going to like this, but I'm recommending that you don't return to the field in full-on Fin mode for the rest of the season."

Furious at his own carelessness, Liam balled his fists and slammed the exam table. "That's two and a half more months, not counting the playoffs. I can't wait that long." No way. No fucking way.

"Getting back out there too soon is a mistake. You don't have the strength or mobility yet. This sprain is going to set you back another two weeks at least."

"I could try doing the stunts and landing on one leg."

"You could, and then you risk falling over because your sense of balance is compromised. You risk inadvertently landing on the injured ankle, too."

"Andy, I can't lose this job. I was supposed to be back on the field by the All-Star game next week."

"That's not going to happen. I'm sorry."

"Can't we wait to see how I am at the end of the week?"

"The initial treatment of a sprain includes resting and protecting the ankle until swelling goes down for about one week. That's followed by a period of one to two weeks of exercise to restore range of motion, strength, and flexibility. It can take several more weeks to several months to gradually return to your normal activities while you continue to exercise. Next week, we can see where you are in terms of motion, strength, and flexibility, but before this sprain happened, you were at about eighty percent of your strength and mobility. You still need several weeks of therapy before I'll be able to clear you to return to the gymnastics activities on the field."

"I don't like that answer. And Ray's not going to like that answer. I need to be able to give him a positive update." Desperation sped through him. "There's still a chance I could go back early, right? If everything heals and progresses by the book?"

Andy sighed. "Yes. There is a chance."

"Then, you'll back me up if I say things are moving in the right direction?"

"I won't lie to Ray, but yes, I can report that things were moving well, that you had a minor setback today, but I expect that you'll be well on your way to fully functioning soon."

"Thanks, Andy. I owe you."

"You can repay me by listening to my advice. I want to see you back on that field just as badly as you want to be there."

He nodded. "I'll listen. Don't worry. See you in a few days."

"I'll text you a copy of my instructions. I know it's a lot to take in. See you in a few days."

Annoyed with the crutches and carefully keeping his bad ankle off the ground, Liam maneuvered into the golf cart and drove to his office. Claire wouldn't have arrived yet. Thankful for the space and quiet to wrap his head around what had happened and make a plan for going forward, he unlocked the door.

Still, as soon as he sat at his desk, he sent her a text checking in. He hadn't seen her since she'd come down with a stomach bug on Thursday. The team had been on a road trip since Wednesday, so she hadn't missed any games. Hopefully, she'd be feeling better for the next day's home game.

A brisk knock pulled him away from his phone. He grabbed his crutches and hobbled to the door. Maybe Andy had somehow realized that Liam needed an ice pack.

No such luck. Raymond stood on the other side.

Raymond glanced at his ankle. "I just saw Andy. He said you had a setback today. That's disappointing. When you first got hurt, I was hoping you would be healed enough to give a great stunt performance at the All-Star game, but I can see that won't be happening."

Liam let his injured foot rest lightly on the floor. "It's only a minor sprain, Ray. Probably only sets me back by a week. Training has been going really well. I'll be able to pick up where I left off." He had no idea if that was true, but he'd say whatever he needed to convince Ray.

"I hope that's all it is. We can only do the current set-up with Fin and Fiona for so long. We don't want the fans to tire of the bit."

Tire of it? Ray was crazy. The fans loved it. "I don't think they're tiring of it. The weekly videos are doing well. Attendance is up for those games because people want to see the next episode of Fin and Fiona before it airs on the web. It's exactly what you hoped would happen."

"Even so, we'll need to see a more mobile Fin out there soon. Andy said you might be ready by mid-August. If not, we'll need to discuss our options."

Liam's blood burned and his heart sank at the veiled threat. If he couldn't do the job, they'd find someone else who could. Or, they'd only keep Claire, either as Fiona, or as a smaller version of Fin. He wasn't sure how their relationship would change if he lost his job to her. Could he handle it, or would resentment build and fester like an infected wound?

As if Ray could read his mind, he asked, "Where *is* Claire?"

"On her way in. We're filming the videos that will be playing during All-Star weekend."

Ray arched a brow at Liam's crutches and bandaged ankle. "Sure you're up to that?"

"No problem at all. You know I'm always about putting the job first." Despite the throbbing pain. "Going back to my recovery, I've been doing great and progressing well with the therapy three times a week, and at home, I'm doing the stretches and exercises three times a day. I'll be ready before mid-August, Ray. You can count on it."

"All right, Liam. Keep me posted." With a brief wave, Ray walked away.

Liam locked the door, then leaned against it, surveying the room. He couldn't lose this. Not to Claire. Not to anyone.

Claire

Claire placed the two pregnancy tests on the bathroom sink and then set the timer in her phone. She walked through her apartment, picking up and setting down books and pillows and rearranging the roses that Liam had given her a few days earlier.

Her period was never late.

Never.

Yet, over a week had passed and she still hadn't gotten it. And maybe the past few days of vomiting wasn't due to a stomach bug.

She couldn't be pregnant. Maybe stress was making her period late. Maybe the stomach virus had thrown her body off.

When she'd suggested that to Savanna, her friend had gently suggested she take a test, just to see.

A series of beeps rang from her phone.

Her heart rate ratcheted faster. The moment of truth. She silenced the alarm and shoved her phone into her pocket. Mouth gone dry, she peered at the results.

Two pink lines on the first test. The word *pregnant* across the display on the second test she'd bought for confirmation.

Her blood froze and her heart struggled to beat. All her muscles turned limp and she began to tremble. She sank onto the toilet lid and covered her face with her hands.

No. No. No. Not now. Not yet.

After being the caregiver for so many years, for keeping her sisters in line and out of harm's way, she deserved a chance to be just Claire.

In an instant, she felt her recently acquired freedom slip away and resentment slid in once more. She and Liam had always been careful and always used a condom, so how had this happened?

Of course, she wanted to have kids *someday*, but after she'd finally had some time to herself. Caring for her sisters had been hard enough. The heavy weight of responsibility would triple with her own child.

Life wasn't fair and she wasn't ready.

Her phone rang, vibrating in her pocket and jolting her off her feet. She scrabbled for it. Lauren's number. Calling again. If she'd hurt herself again...

She'd better answer.

"What's up?"

"Can you drive me to gymnastics? I need to be there in an hour."

Huffing a sigh, she dragged her hands over her face. So not what she needed right now. "Fine. But be ready to leave when I arrive. I have to go to work right after that and can't be late."

Great. Just great.

She swept the tests into the trash.

Queasiness interfered with her concentration on the road. When she pulled up in front of the family home, she blinked at the number of cars in the driveway—Amanda's Escalade, Jen's Jeep, Krissy's Fiat, Ginger's Corvette, and Dad's Range Rover.

Lauren dashed out the front door with her gym bag thrown over her shoulder and a bright smile on her face. She tugged the passenger door open. "Hi."

"Hold up. Why did you call me? Everyone is home."

Her sister shrugged. "What's the big deal? When you lived here, you used to drive me all the time."

Damn it. Annoyance sizzling through her muscles, Claire squeezed the steering wheel. "Yeah. When I lived here. I don't anymore. I haven't for a few months. You have five people who are capable of driving you. There was no reason to call me."

"We should get going. Coach doesn't like it when we're late." Lauren climbed into the seat and turned on the radio.

Claire switched it off. "Does everyone else know that you called me?"

"Not Dad. He's still asleep. He got home pretty late last night."

"Did you ask the others to drive you before calling me?"

"They were arguing about who was supposed to do it, so I said I'd call you and they stopped."

Claire turned off the engine. "Let's go. We're having a family meeting."

"But I'm gonna be late."

"Too damn bad." She slammed her door shut and stalked

up the path. No freaking way would she let herself be walked on any longer.

Her sisters were sprawled across the living room and kitchen. The rooms were a mess once again. Claire strode to the center of the living room as the front door slammed.

Lauren bolted past her, shoving into the kitchen. She dropped her bag onto the floor, seething. "Someone better drive me to the gym."

Krissy raised her gaze from her phone. "I thought Claire was doing it."

"I'm not doing it." Rolling her eyes, Claire turned to address all of her sisters. "She shouldn't have called me and you shouldn't have let her. You're all sitting around here. There's no reason one of you can't drive her."

Amanda and Jen opened their mouths, but Claire cut them off with a wave of her hand. "I don't know what the hell is going on, but before I moved out we all had a talk about how you guys would have to work together to handle chores and schedules and driving Lauren around. In the three months that I've been gone, you've called me a ton of times asking for my help with things that I later learned you all could have and should have handled. I don't expect you to track chores and schedules the way I did, but you have to do better than this."

Stony silence settled over the rooms. Five glares met her. Then Amanda stood. "We don't need you lecturing us. You're not our mother."

She stiffened. Justified heat bloomed from her chest and raced to the ends of every limb. Amanda was right. She wasn't their mother and trying to fill that hole stopped right now. "I've always tried to make up for Mom not being here, but you're right, I'm not her. You guys want to live in chaos, fighting, casting blame and shirking responsibilities, so go ahead. But from now on, don't call me unless one of you is bleeding, and even then, only if you can't get a hold of each other or Dad."

She let herself out of the house, blinking away tears as she hurried to her car.

Halfway to the ballpark, her stomach heaved once, twice, again. *Oh, no.* Claire jerked the car into a shopping center parking lot and thrust her door open just in time to avoid creating a mess in her car.

Wiping her hand across her mouth, she sagged against the seat. She'd better do some research on handling morning sickness.

Her phone pinged with a text alert. She lifted it slowly, steeling herself for a message from one of her sisters. Liam's name, instead, made her smile.

Liam: Hope you're feeling better today. If you're not, just call. We can film the video later this week. See you soon.

He thought she had a stomach bug. In all the drama with her sisters, she hadn't thought past the shock of the pregnancy to the fact that it affected him too.

She hadn't a clue how to tell him the news when she could barely believe it herself.

Claire wandered through the crowd of All-Star fans at the ballpark. Hot dogs, nachos, and fried foods scented the air and kept her in a permanent state of nausea. In the week since she'd learned of the pregnancy, working every night at the park, being bombarded by those scents, had taken its toll. Throwing up three to five times a day wasn't any fun and the home remedies for morning sickness weren't working. She needed to call her doctor.

She ducked through the door leading to the quiet inner

hallways and breathed in deep to expel the offending odors from her nose and lungs.

Raymond had asked her to stop by his office after she'd completed her hour of posing for pictures with the fans. Perhaps he'd realized that she'd scaled back her on-field routine this week. She hadn't had a choice. Cartwheels and flips were difficult when her body was exhausted and drained and queasy all the time. She needed to get her nausea under control, otherwise she might not be able to perform the stunts at all.

But she couldn't share the real reason with him. Not when Liam didn't know yet.

Between his upset over the setback of the sprained ankle, the preparations for the All-Star game, and their increased appearances for the influx of press, media, and fans, she hadn't found the right time to tell him. She couldn't exactly blurt out "hey, we're having a baby" the same way she'd tell him that they needed to head to the field.

She stopped in her office, striped off her costume, and left a message for her doctor. On her way to Ray's office, she sipped a can of ginger ale Liam had found at a specialty store. He thought she still had a stomach bug.

They needed to talk. After tonight's game, they had two days off. She'd find a way to tell him tomorrow.

She stopped in front of Ray's open door and he waved her in. "Claire, have a seat. If you don't mind, please close the door behind you."

If Ray mentioned her lackluster performances, she'd blame the stomach bug. The scent of his cologne wasn't doing anything to help her nausea. Hopefully, the meeting would be quick.

He offered her a warm smile. "We're very pleased with your performance so far, and the fans love you."

Oh, good. Her tightened stomach eased. "Thanks, Ray. I'm really enjoying being here."

"You were hired as a temporary employee but we'd like to make you a permanent part of the talent roster. And raise your salary to be more commensurate with your popularity and level of success."

"Wow. That's great. Thank you." Tears threatened to form and she bit the inside of her cheek until the urge passed. Crazy hormones. If her doctor was right about her due date, she'd deliver in mid-February. She might have to miss part of Spring Training, but she'd work it out then.

"That brings me to the other reason I wanted to talk to you. We want a fully functioning mascot team. Does your old gymnastics coach have any students that are close to Liam's height and build?"

"I don't know. Why?" Her stomach sank as the reason for his question sank in.

"We can only play the Fin and Fiona videos and have Fin riding around in a golf cart for so long. The fans want to see Fin doing the flips and stunts. We need him back."

"Liam said he should be ready before mid-August."

"If so, that's great, but that's a month away and he's not even back at physical therapy yet. I can't wait until the last minute to replace him again, so I'm beginning to look for a potential candidate now. I'd appreciate if you can ask your coach to keep an eye out for someone along his size. The costumes set us back about ten grand so I'd like to keep using Liam's as long as I can."

"If Liam loses this job, it'll crush him."

"Claire, I don't feel happy about this either, but I need to look at the bottom line." Ray shuffled papers on his desk and avoided eye contact. "If we can't find anyone else, we could try the guy who took part in the audition who was close to

Liam's build. You said you used to coach gymnastics. Maybe you could work with him on his mechanics."

"I…" She stalled. Oh no. No way. She didn't want any parts in any plans to replace Liam. "He looked like a total beginner. Expecting him to reach Liam's level of capability in a manner of days or weeks isn't reasonable."

"But you are willing to help train him if we can't find someone more suitable?" He looked at her expectantly.

Feeling every bit the traitor, without a choice she nodded. Her stomach quivered, only this time it wasn't morning sickness. "I'll help."

"Excellent. We highly value employees who are committed to helping the organization. Let me know what your coach says. I'll check in with that prospect. I'll need you involved in making the selection."

If Liam lost his job as Fin and learned she had a hand in it —they'd be through. Her heart would break. And her baby would grow up in a broken home. Just like her. Totally unacceptable. She squeezed her hands together, ready to plead for him. "But, you won't actually give anyone the job of Fin as long as Liam is able to come back in a month?"

"Right. I have a progress meeting scheduled with Andy and Liam on August eighteenth. If Liam is good to go, we'll continue with him as Fin. If he's not, then the new Fin will take the field at the next home game the following week."

A bout of nausea hit out of nowhere. Claire quickly rose and shook Ray's hand, again promising to help, and then bolted out of the room and to the nearest restroom.

If she didn't help out, Ray might choose to replace her too. After all, there were several gymnasts of her size and now, Ray knew who to contact.

If she couldn't get a handle on her nausea, they could let her go for not being able to perform the duties she'd been hired to do. They were ready to replace Liam and he'd been there for years. They would have even less loyalty to her, as new as she was. If she lost this job, she wouldn't be able to handle a full-time gymnastics gig as her pregnancy progressed. And even if she landed an office job, she'd feel guilty about taking maternity leave only a few months after starting. What if she had to move home? Return to her selfish sisters and all their whining.

It was best to go along and do whatever Ray wanted her to do. She couldn't let anything jeopardize her position. Not now. Not when she wasn't the only one depending on her.

CHAPTER EIGHTEEN

SLADE

Slade woke up to early afternoon sunlight streaming in the bedroom window and a note from Savanna propped against a bottle of water.

Drink me. Rehydrate. xo, Savanna.

Not a bad idea after a long night out celebrating his All-Star appearance. He rolled out of bed, stretched his muscles, and turned on the TV. The baseball channel played highlights from the previous night's All-Star game. He pulled on clothes and chugged the bottle, automatically critiquing himself when his image and stats flashed onto the screen.

He'd more than made up for his abysmal performance in front of his parents. During the Home Run Derby, he'd launched ball after ball into the stands, winning the event, and had scored two runs in the All-Star game, helping his team to a win. James and Tiffany had been in the stands for both events.

Savanna had too. And even though she'd stayed out late with Liam and Dom and him, she'd had to get up early for work. He grabbed his phone to text her a thanks for the water and found one from Dom, checking in and making plans for dinner, and one from Tiffany, asking if he could meet her later at her home.

He fired off responses, sent the text to Savanna, and wandered into the kitchen.

Liam sat at the counter, devouring half of a huge submarine sandwich. Mouth full, he raised his brows at Slade and pushed over the other half.

"Thanks." Slade popped a coffee pod into the single-cup brewer and then tugged the plate closer.

"Dom sent a text. Dinner tonight." Liam waved his phone in the air. "I'm meeting with Andy soon so he can check my ankle. If he pronounces it healed, I'll get cleared to return to PT. I think he will. It doesn't hurt anymore."

"I'll buy the first round tonight to celebrate." Grinning at his friend, Slade twisted to grab his coffee. "Tiffany wants me to stop by this afternoon."

"Did she say why?"

He shook his head and bit into his sandwich. Maybe his bio mom wanted to chat because they hadn't had a chance to talk after the game. Or maybe she was trying to start a ritual, an afternoon coffee visit much like Savanna's Sunday lunches with her parents. That was fine with him.

Maybe he needed to start one with Liam. With both of them in relationships, they didn't spend as much one-on-one time as before, and he missed his buddy. Kicking back, he enjoyed his breakfast with Liam and the easy friendship that had been a constant in his life for so long.

After Liam left for his appointment, Slade headed out. The weather was gorgeous, so he opted for the Harley.

He was riding high when he knocked on Tiffany's door, ready to spend some time with her.

When she answered the door, he could see the tension in her pale face. Shoulders hunched and wringing her hands, she led him to the sun room. "Thanks for coming over."

"Sure. Is anyone else home?"

"James took the kids to the beach. I told him I wanted to do this alone."

Slade lowered himself onto a small wooden chair. She looked too tense. "So…"

Tiffany sat on the middle couch cushion. Close but not too close. She pressed her lips together and then let out a low, slow breath. "There's something I need to tell you. I've wrestled with whether I should, but I feel guilty, and I don't want there to be any secrets between us. Because if it ever did come out, I want you to hear it from me."

His gut tightened. Slade leaned forward, forearms on his thighs. "What's wrong?"

"A year after the adoption, when I was sixteen, I overheard someone at my parents' church gossiping about how I'd gotten pregnant at fifteen and that Jeannette had adopted you. I learned her name then, but nothing else. After that, I stopped attending services there. When I saw Jeannette's obituary in the paper five years later, I contacted a lawyer about trying to get you back."

He tensed. Not what he'd expected to hear on his drive over. Instinctually, he guarded his heart, ready for it to break. "So, what happened? How did I end up with Liz?"

"I was twenty-two and pregnant with Melanie. My husband at the time was a… a very difficult person. Emotionally abusive. But back then I hadn't yet found the courage to leave him. He refused to raise another man's son. It was too hard to fight him. I didn't have much money or enough to support myself, let alone you and a baby. So I gave in."

He stood, his legs shaky and his mind racing. Once again, he felt like the boy living with his aunt, a flat out inconvenience. "You gave in. Do you have any idea what my life was like? I lost the only mother I'd known, and then was sent to live with her aunt, a woman in her fifties who had no desire to raise a child but did it for the money she'd receive to take care of me. She gave me a roof over my head, but that was it. I was basically left alone. I grew up unwanted, regardless."

"You didn't tell us that part when you talked about living with Liz."

"You said you'd hoped and prayed for years that I was happy and loved. Letting you think that I had been seemed kinder than telling you the truth."

She flattened a hand over her heart. "I'm sorry. Back then, I was still young. So scared."

Scared. The one word pushed his button. Damn in, he'd been scared. "You don't think I was young and scared at six, when my mother was suddenly gone? Or when I was growing up in Liz's house, knowing she didn't love me or want me there? Or when I turned eighteen, and had to get the hell out because that's when the money cut off?"

Tiffany's eyes widened and tears spilled down her cheeks. "I'm horrified. I don't know what to say. I thought I was giving you a better life."

Anger and hurt swirled as old memories surfaced and unleashed fresh pain. "Well, you didn't. It was hell. The loneliness and feelings of worthlessness swallow you whole. Even now, do you have any idea what my relationships are like? How hard it is to trust people? How long it takes me before I believe someone isn't going to disappear?"

"I'm sorry. I'm so sorry."

"Yeah. I am too." The urge to move, to leave, was too strong to resist. He looked for his leather jacket, then realized he'd never taken it off. "I need to go."

She didn't say anything, or if she did, he didn't hear her.

He started up his bike and the engine's roar drowned out his thoughts.

As he traveled back to L.A., the familiar ache opened in his chest with the need to do something daring, to feel that burst of adrenaline flowing through him to take away his pain. He'd held off for weeks, on Dom's advice, and because being with Savanna calmed that ache. But Tiffany's revelation, that she'd abandoned him twice, rocked him to his core.

He needed something big to fix it. Something he'd never done before.

His motorcycle swung into the lot of Savanna's apartment building before he realized what he'd done. Once there, he couldn't leave without seeing her. He parked next to her car and cut the engine.

She must have heard his arrival or seen him coming. The door swung open before he knocked.

The smile fell away from her face when she met his gaze. "What's wrong?"

He reached for her hand. "Let's go BASE jumping."

Savanna

Savanna blinked at his request and tugged his hand until he came inside. "Are you crazy? I'm not jumping off the side of a cliff with nothing but a baggy suit as my means to the ground."

"You can do it with a parachute too. From a bridge or a skyscraper. My buddy at the skydiving place can hook us up."

"Isn't BASE jumping illegal in most places in the US?"

"Only if you get caught. Come on, what do you say?" He

inclined his head toward the door. His face worked in a way she'd never seen it, a mixture of hurt and anger and fear.

"No." This time she was drawing the proverbial line in the sand. "Lots of people have died during a jump. And you shouldn't go anywhere in your state, let alone risk your life. Or mine."

"I'm not in a state."

"You are. You're talking fast, more agitated than excited. You're really keyed up." She gingerly laid a hand on his arm, like she would a new patient in the hospital. "Why don't you tell me what's wrong instead?"

His eyes closed as she touched him, but after a minute, he shook his head and stepped back. "I need to go."

Now he was starting to worry her. "Slade. You came here for a reason. Talk to me. Please."

Sighing, he stared at the ceiling like he hoped the words would appear there. "Tiffany had the chance to get me back after my adoptive mom died. But her husband didn't want me. So, yeah. You know how that turned out."

"I'm sorry. So sorry." She reached for him again, but he remained stiff, vibrating with energy.

"Anyway, I'm dying here. Let's go. I need to burn some energy. We can do the jump off one of the skyscrapers in downtown L.A. We can be down there in—"

"No. I'm not doing it and I don't want you to do it either."

His head shot up. "What?"

Fear gripped her heart as tight as she squeezed his hand. "It's too dangerous. I've never asked you not to do something. But I'm asking now."

He reached for her other hand and locked them together. "You don't have to do the jump, but I need you there with me."

"I'm here. Right now. *Talk* to me. We can figure out how to help you together. You don't have to jump either."

"I need to do it. You don't understand."

Realization dawned at the pain on his face. "I think I do. You take chances like this because you think no one cares about you."

"That's not—"

"Don't you dare tell me it's not true. I see you right now. Something happened to hurt you and this is how you handle it."

His withdrew his hands and the absence of his heat chilled her skin. "That's a pretty astute opinion from someone who's afraid of everything."

"Not wanting to take ridiculous risks isn't being afraid of everything." Her mind raced searching for the right words to keep him grounded, but her heart beat so fast that she couldn't concentrate. He'd aimed his words right at her softest spot and hit it. "You make it sound like I'm afraid of my own shadow. That's crazy and you know it. Redirecting the attention away from how you're choosing to handle your hurt doesn't change a thing."

His eyes flickered with vulnerability. "You don't know what you're talking about."

"Fine. Deny it all you want. I'm asking you not to do this because I worry about something happening to you."

"Worrying about something doesn't help. All it does is create crazy what-if scenarios in your head, ninety-nine percent of which won't come true."

"Maybe so. But that doesn't change the fact that I'd be devastated if something happened to you. How's that for a reason?"

His gaze held hers, eyes direct, face impassive. "If I don't do this, what's next? You'll ask me to stop skydiving or racing fast cars? I am who I am and I've never hidden that from you. I can't stop doing things I love just because they make you uncomfortable."

The quiet words cut deep. But the reverse was true for her. "And I can't do things that make me uncomfortable just because you love them."

They stared at each other for a long moment and Savanna could see this same argument and occurrence happening over and over for the rest of their relationship.

"I can't watch you do something self-destructive. It's too scary. I don't like it." She sighed out her frustration at not being able to get through to him. "It's not only about the BASE jumping. It's how we approach everything. We're too different and it's time we admitted it."

His eyes narrowed. "What are you getting at?"

Her chest hurt, but that made sense. Her heart was breaking. She took a breath, licked dry lips, and opened her mouth. "That we're too different. You're swimming with sharks and I can't even conquer the diving board. You're jumping out of planes and I can't stand flying. You're living in a penthouse and I don't like living above the second floor. I've been thinking for a while and this right here is one more instance that proves I'm right."

"Right about what?"

"Us being together is a mistake."

His mouth worked open and he rubbed his hand over his hair. "I don't think it is."

"You need someone as fearless as you. And that's not me. I don't want to fight every time you suggest doing something. Or us growing to resent each other because you think I'm holding you back or I think you're pushing too far."

"I've never pushed you too far." His immediate response was as strong as steel.

"Not yet. But I can see it coming. Like with the BASE jumping. I don't want you to do it. It's so dangerous."

"It's not—"

"But you're going to do it anyway, regardless of whatever I say or how scared I am. This isn't the same as you leaving socks in the middle of the floor and me complaining about it. This is you doing something reckless and I can't handle it."

"Come on, Savanna…" He stepped closer.

"I don't want to deal with carrying around the additional weight of worrying about you over things like this. It's too much. I don't think we should see each other anymore."

Slade's eyes widened. His lips parted and then closed and he rubbed a hand over his hair again. "I see. I'm too reckless for you. It's all about your fears and none of mine."

"Please. You don't have any fears."

"That's where you're wrong." He glanced at his helmet, looking lost for a second, before an odd light came into his eyes. "I always told you that I'd protect you. And if protecting you means leaving you alone so you don't have to worry about me, then I'll do what you want. I need to go."

He turned and walked out.

Savanna collapsed against the back of the couch, replaying their conversation over the pounding beats of her heart.

A few seconds later, his motorcycle roared to life.

She crossed to the window and drew back the curtain. He tore down the street. His figure grew smaller and smaller, until it melted into the traffic.

Savanna let the curtain fall into place.

Ending things was for the best. But she hadn't expected it to hurt so much.

CHAPTER NINETEEN

LIAM

He could start back up with PT again next week. The thought replayed itself over and over in Liam's mind as he walked away from Andy's office, happier than he'd been in days. His ankle was still a little sore, but he barely felt the ache.

He couldn't wait to tell Claire the news. He exited the stadium, the stark quiet a contrast to the revelry of the previous evening's All-Star game.

"Liam." Raymond waved as he set the alarm on his car and approached the building.

"Hey, Ray." Liam slowed to a stop. "Good news, Andy gave me the okay to return to PT next week."

Brows raised, Ray smiled and nodded. "Good, good. But take all the time you need to heal. Claire and I are working on lining up an alternative for you if you can't make it back."

"Wait, what?" He couldn't have heard that correctly.

"She's on board to coach the new hire if needed too. We really lucked out with her."

Liam shook his head, confusion and anger and betrayal battling for dominance. "But I am going to make it back. Mid-August, remember?"

"I hope so. But I need a contingency plan in place. Just like the team. Every position has at least one backup. You understand that."

"But I also understand if a replacement plays better than the injured guy, the replacement becomes the starter, even after the original guy is healed." He couldn't lose his job, but it seemed like his time as Fin was slipping through his fingers and he couldn't grab hold.

Ray held up his hands. "Relax, Liam. You're thinking too far ahead. Just worry about getting yourself better."

Not exactly a *don't worry, the job will always be yours.* "Well, that's reassuring. Thanks a lot, Ray." Sarcasm sharpened his tone and Liam walked away before saying something he'd regret. His professionalism didn't extend very far. He felt blindsided. But Ray had said Claire had a role in the alternative mascot plan, too.

He needed answers.

Now.

Twenty minutes later, he knocked on Claire's door.

When she opened it, some of his anger receded as his concern surged forward. Purple smudges under her eyes, pale skin, and a wan smile on her lips, she hugged her arms around her middle. "Did I miss something? I wasn't expecting to see you until later tonight."

"I just had an interesting conversation with Ray." He studied her expression. Sure enough, she looked guilty.

"Oh?"

With that, his hurt doubled. "Any reason you didn't tell me about your involvement in lining up a replacement for me?"

She backed up, probably as much shying away from her guilt as letting him inside. "Come in."

He strode to the middle of the living room. "Well?"

"Ray stressed that he needed a fully functioning mascot unit and asked if my old gymnastics coach had any students that were close to your height and build."

"Does she?"

"I didn't ask her yet. He only broached the subject with me yesterday."

Frustration crawled over his skin like an itch he couldn't scratch. "Are you going to ask her?"

She became intently interested in the swirling lines of color on her area rug.

The lack of response spoke volumes. He crossed his arms over his chest. "Did you tell him no?"

Pleading blue eyes raised to meet his gaze. "I couldn't do that, Liam. I can't have him thinking I'm not a team player."

"*We're* a team. You and me. At least I thought we were. But you're willing to be an active participant in the hiring of my replacement? And you were doing it behind my back?" He shook his head. Gutted. She'd lured him in then slit him open the second he'd become vulnerable.

"What was I supposed to do?"

"You were supposed to put me before the job."

"You've always said the job comes first."

"I would never put it before you."

"I wonder." Her hands moved to rest on her hips. "I mean, the day we met, you and Slade made sure that you were going to stick around, even after I was brought in."

"That was different."

"How?"

"This job is more than just a job to me. It's who I am. Cheering up sick kids, making the fans happy, that fuels me. I'm doing all I ever wanted to do, and what I was meant to do." He jabbed his finger into his chest while he paced in front of her. "I need you to go to bat for me. To tell him no, that we can come up with something else while I recover."

"If I'm not helpful, I could lose my job too. I can't let that happen right now." She pressed her hand to her stomach. "I can't tell Ray no."

He had to get out of here. No question, his heart split apart. No other explanation for the intense pain twisting in his chest. She might as well have shot him. His worst fears, made a million times worse. Betrayal lanced through his soul. His chest hurt like she'd literally stabbed him in the heart. "I can't do this."

"What are you talking about?"

He waved his hand between them. "This. Us."

"You're breaking up with me?" Disbelief turned her sweet face pale, but what had she expected from him?

"I need someone who has my back. Who I can trust to fight for me just as hard as I'd fight for her. Who loves me just as much as I—" He stopped. The words didn't matter. Not now. Saying *I love you* didn't change a thing. If she really loved *him*, she wouldn't be able to hurt him this way.

"But, Liam, I—"

"You what? Need to look out for yourself? Just like the former co-workers you told me about. I get it. Really. It's not personal, it's business, right?" He moved toward the door. "I'll see you at Friday's game." *If he still had his job by then.*

What the hell was he going to do if he really lost it?

He yanked the door closed behind him and stomped to his car on an ankle that still wasn't right. Slamming into his car, he cursed and pounded his fist against the steering wheel. He'd been fighting for his job with all he had, and that might still not be enough to keep it. Hot bolts of anger surged through him and the ache in his chest spread, making breathing difficult.

His phone chirped with messages from Slade, Dom, and Adam.

Slade: Going BASE jumping. Now. Need my buds. Address below. Get here.

Dom: Slade, what the hell is wrong with you? This falls under the reckless things you're supposed to be avoiding. DO. NOT. JUMP.

Adam: FYI, it's illegal. Both the team and the cops will have your ass for it. Dom and I are heading over now.

Liam paused with his thumbs over the keypad. The more he thought about it, the more he liked Slade's idea.

Liam: On my way. Slade, wait for me. I'll do it with you.

He tossed his phone onto the seat and turned onto the freeway. Might as well jump too. After all, he had nothing left to lose.

Slade

The ache in his stomach hurt worse than the time he'd taken a ninety-mile-an-hour fastball to the gut. She didn't want him anymore. He downed a shot of whiskey. After the initial burn, a chill seeped into his skin.

Worthless. Unlovable. Unwanted.

The words that had repeated themselves in his head all his life replayed over and over. He couldn't deal. Not now. The only thing that made sense was getting away.

Slade pushed away from the bar and strode toward the door of the pub. He had a date with the skyscraper across the street.

Liam, Dom, and Adam burst into the room. Dom's dark

eyes snapped between anger and concern. "Slade, what the hell?"

Seeing his friends set off another wave of unrest that skittered just under his skin. Why did they still hang around him? Was it only a matter of time until he did something to push them away too? He rubbed his hands over his face, and then looked at them, helpless to admit what he needed.

Dom's heavy hand settled on his shoulder. "Slade. What's going on?"

Slade looked from Dom, to Adam, to Liam. How to explain all that had transpired? "First off, Tiffany let on that she had the chance to get me back after Jeannette died, and but the challenges she encountered outweighed how much she wanted me."

"Shit, Slade." Liam let out a low whistle.

Dom patted him once more before moving his hand away. "I'm sorry."

"Did she actually say that?" Arms crossed, Adam raised a brow.

"No, but it sure as hell feels that way. There were challenges there, but come on, man. I was her *son*. You know how I grew up."

Slade looked out the window. The city pulsed with its own energy and he felt an answering beat in his blood. "Savanna dumped me. I'd been waiting for the thing that would push her away, and asking her to come do this with me was apparently it. Doesn't matter that I fucking needed her. Needed to know that I wasn't alone. That she loved—" His throat thickened. He rubbed his hand over his face again and focused on pushing those feelings down and locking them away. When he had a handle on his control, he looked up. "Time to jump."

"Slade, no. That's too big a risk." Dom's hands covered

his shoulders and he turned Slade toward the door. "I'm pulling the big brother card. Let's go home."

"We're not brothers. I don't have any family. I don't have anyone." Drawing away from Dom, he closed in on himself. Sooner or later, everyone would leave.

"Bullshit." Dom glared at him. "You'll always have me. And these guys. You know that. We love you, even when you're being an idiot."

Slade met his gaze, swallowing hard. Gratitude, disbelief, love, and hope tumbled through him.

Dom slung his arm over Slade's shoulder and pulled him into a hug. "You're family to me. Don't forget that. I know I won't."

Slade clung tight. Tears burned his eyes. He hadn't cried in years, not since he'd been a kid, afraid and alone. But here he was, close to losing it in the middle of a bar in the middle of the city on display for anyone to see.

Adam's hand covered his other shoulder. "You'll always have us."

Liam rested his hand on Slade's head and then he threw his arms around the group. "Slade, you know you're the brother I never had. I won't let anyone break up the act. No matter what, that bond won't break."

Slade raised his head. "Were you really going to jump with me, Li?"

Liam nodded. "A little dangerous for me, but I'd do it because you needed me."

"But your ankle. You could re-injure it. It's not fully healed." The depth of Liam's friendship was as deep as the ocean. As far as he'd go for Slade, Slade needed to go just as far to protect him. "We're not jumping. Dom's right, let's go home."

"Thank you." Dom's labored sigh felt like a load off his shoulders, too. His bud steered them toward the door.

Home meant the bar section of the restaurant on the first floor of their apartment building. They took up one side of the bar, with Slade sitting between Dom and Liam, and Adam on Dom's other side.

Dom ordered the first round of shots. "To Slade, for common sense prevailing."

"It wasn't common sense. It was you guys." He knocked back his drink, feeling the love for his buddies. "My crew."

Liam toasted him. "Now that Claire and I are over, you guys are all that I have."

Slade whipped around so fast his chair spun. "You're over, too? What the fuck happened?"

"Ray wants a fully mobile, stunt-ready Fin by mid-August. He and Claire are searching for a replacement for me now, just in case, so the new guy can slip in right away if I'm not ready to go then."

Torn between offering comfort and getting angry on his friend's behalf, Slade patted Liam's shoulder. "That sucks."

"She wouldn't say no to Ray. She's picking my replacement and training the bastard. This all took place behind my back."

Adam motioned to the bartender. "I think we'll need another round."

Liam rubbed his hand over the back of his neck. "If I lose the job…"

"You won't." Dom's firm voice ordered him to believe it.

"But if I do…" Rounded, wounded, desolate eyes met theirs.

Adam passed around the fresh drinks. "Then, we'll just give you a shit ton of money for watching the dogs."

Liam's laughter followed Adam's calm, matter of fact solution. "Dude, be serious."

"I am. You know we'll help you out."

Slade slung his arm around Liam's shoulder. "I always have your back. You know you can count on us."

"I know. I'm lucky."

"Me too." They clinked glasses and downed the next round. Warm fuzziness spread through his joints.

A while later, Dom stood. "You guys are going upstairs after this, right? No going out and doing anything stupid?"

"Upstairs," Slade agreed. He one-arm hugged Dom and lost his balance, catching himself before he fell off the stool.

"All right. We'll check in with you tomorrow." Adam hugged Slade and then Liam.

Arm in arm with Liam, Slade watched Adam and Dom walk out of the bar. "Ready to head up?"

Liam laughed. "You're weaving from side to side. I'll help you walk."

"You're the one weaving. I'll help *you*." Grinning at Liam, Slade bumped his shoulder and knocked them both into the bar.

"Don't fall on me, man."

They made it to their apartment without incident. Slade unlocked the door. "Another drink?"

"Let's do it." Liam held on to the wall on his way to the kitchen.

Slade grabbed the scotch and glasses. They sat side by side with the bottle between them. "I'm sorry about Claire."

"And I'm sorry about Savanna." Liam swallowed his shot.

Slade studied the amber liquid swirling in his glass. "I love her. And I messed it up."

"It takes two to mess things up." Liam poured them another round.

He pondered that wisdom for a moment. "That true for you and Claire too?"

His friend pushed the glass aside and sat, elbows on the counter and hands in his hair. "I guess I didn't really give her a chance to explain why she did what she did."

"So, talk to her."

"I don't know that she'll talk to me now."

He hated seeing his friend so upset. Even if he'd wrecked his own relationship, maybe he could somehow save Liam and Claire's. "Maybe I can help."

Liam raised his head. "How?"

"I don't know. But we have the whole night and half a bottle of scotch. We'll think of something."

CHAPTER TWENTY

CLAIRE

Claire opened the door and waved Savanna into her apartment. They could wallow in their misery together or spend a few hours trashing love and watching sappy, romantic comedies, whichever her friend wanted. "I'm glad you're here."

Savanna looked just as drained as she felt. "How are you feeling?"

"Pretty bad. My doctor recommended a different pre-natal vitamin and a vitamin B-6 supplement. I haven't gotten sick in a few hours, but I'm not feeling much better yet."

"Did you tell your dad about the baby? Maybe he can ask some of the OB's at the hospital about morning sickness cures if the new remedies don't work."

"No one knows about the baby. I'll probably tell my dad soon though." She hadn't talked to him or her sisters in over a week. Not since the fight.

Savanna held out the bag she'd brought. "If you're feeling daring, we can have ginger ale and crackers for dinner."

"I can't feed you that. You'll want real food." But she

gratefully accepted the soda and crackers and set them in the kitchen.

"I didn't want to risk cooking and you getting sick from the smell. I'll be fine with a sandwich or something."

"Help yourself to anything in the fridge. Or, there's a deli and a few restaurants close by."

The knock on the door startled her. She wasn't expecting anyone else. Would Liam come back to fight again? Maybe she could try to explain this time. She shrugged at Savanna and checked through the security lens. "It's my dad."

Surprise shifted to worry. If something bad had happened and no one had called her… She tugged the door open. "Dad? Is everything okay?"

He bent to hug her. "I was on my way home from work and thought I'd drop in. Is now a bad time? I want to talk to you about your sisters."

Savanna introduced herself and then walked to the front door. "I'll run down to that specialty Italian market and find us something for dinner."

Dad waited until Savanna was gone. "I heard about what happened last week. Your sisters had a big fight about it today."

Unsure of what to say, Claire gestured to the kitchen. "Can I get you a drink?"

"I can't stay long. Lauren is at a friend's house and needs a ride home soon. With you not at home anymore, I can really see everything you handled. I'm here to apologize, for myself and for them. And believe me, they're sending a huge apology."

"For what?"

"For their behavior last week and for all the years that you stepped up and fulfilled extra roles."

"Dad, I didn't mind. I wanted to help."

Dad shook his head and leaned against the counter. "Your mother wanted a houseful of kids because she was lonely. Then, after we had all of you, she was overwhelmed. We didn't communicate well back then. When she left, I didn't see it coming. But I still don't see how she could leave you guys without a backwards glance. I thought the best thing I could do was provide for you. Having Grandma there for the first few years helped, but by then, you were so responsible. I didn't let you be a kid. I didn't insist on it, and I'm sorry. You had too much responsibility from too young an age and for too many years."

"It's all right."

Placing his hand on her shoulder, he shook his head again. "It was too much. You were Lauren's age when Grandma died, and from then on, you held down chores and babysitting, basically being the mom from then until you moved out a few months ago."

"In the beginning, I was scared you'd feel like Mom did, that we were all a burden, and want to leave us too or worse, somehow send us to live with her."

"Never. I'm sorry you overheard her say that. You girls are my joy. I know I missed out on a lot. That's my fault. I really thought that working so much and being able to give you all the lessons and sports camps and classes and cars would make up for Mom leaving. I wish I could go back in time. I'd do a lot differently. But the only thing I can do is go forward and be more present for you all now. I want to come to one of your games and watch you entertain the crowd."

Her sensitive stomach shrunk and knotted. Maybe she'd finally feel better if she shared her news. "I'm not sure how much longer I'll be doing that… Dad, I'm pregnant. And I can't stop throwing up. I can't do the job they need me to do if I'm too exhausted and weak to perform."

"I can't believe my baby is having a baby." He hugged her, and then guided her to a chair. "How far along are you?"

"Still early in the first trimester."

"Have you talked to you obstetrician about the nausea?"

"She started me on a different pre-natal vitamin today."

"If it doesn't work, there are lots of treatment options. Your mother had bad nausea with every pregnancy."

"I don't want to be anything like her." She recoiled at the thought. "Dad, I'm scared. What if I resent this baby the way Mom resented me? I don't want to, but what if it's somehow ingrained?"

He sat beside her. "I'll tell you something. Every single one of you is a blessing to me. I really believe that your mother thought so too. There's six years between you and Amanda, and then the rest of the pack came very close together—four more kids within a five-year span. It was a lot to handle. If I'd done a better job, your mother might not have left. Deep down, she resented *me*, not you. I'm the reason she left."

She may have been relieved to share the burden, but felt worse for her dad. He'd been all alone since Mom left, too. She wasn't sure what to say to ease the guilt and regret in his voice and on his face. She patted his hand. "I think we all would have been a handful, regardless."

"I didn't realize you were seeing anyone. Is the father someone I know?"

She shook her head. "His name is Liam. He's the other mascot. I screwed up things there. It's a mess. He's pretty upset with me right now. And he doesn't know about the baby yet."

"So, you'll work it out. If you love each other and want to work at your relationship, you can fix anything. And if things don't work out, you won't be alone. You'll always have your sisters and me. You know you can always come back home. You took care of all of us for a long time. It's time we take care of you."

"Thanks, Dad." She hugged him, happy to cling to the promise that she could count on him. For the first time in a week she didn't feel like she was in this all alone.

Knowing she would have support from her family, she wasn't as scared about facing the future.

But, she still needed to talk to Liam and somehow fix the mess she'd created.

Savanna

Savanna curled up on one end of Claire's couch, mug of tea in hand. "I haven't seen any news alerts about a man falling to his death while BASE jumping, so I guess Slade's fine."

Claire sat on the opposite end, cross-legged, sipping her ginger ale. "You could text him. Make sure he's okay."

"No. I lost that right when I ended things." She picked at the fringe hanging off the throw blanket on the back of the couch. "I…"

"Do you want to talk about it?"

Sighing, she dropped the blanket. "I didn't think I had a choice. All I could see was him rushing off to do this crazy, dangerous stunt without taking my fears, my feelings for him into account. I know I worry a lot, but I've made a conscious effort to be better. I even pause to consider the positive aspects instead of immediately imaging the worst possible what-ifs. But things like this… with him… I love him and I don't want to lose him to a horrible accident from an adventure gone wrong. But then I ended up losing him anyway."

It hurt. An ache in her stomach that reached into her soul.

She sipped her tea. How would she handle seeing him at the next Wishes Granted event? Her chest tightened at the thought. Desperate for a distraction, she gestured to Claire. "Let's talk about something else. Your coloring looks better. And you're keeping down that chicken and pasta."

"Yay for me." Smiling, Claire lifted her soda in mock toast. "I'm feeling better. Not back to normal, but not like I'm going to fall over anymore."

"So what happened with Liam? When I called, you said you guys had a fight about the job?"

"He's so angry. And I don't know how to fix it."

Savanna's phone, resting on the arm of the couch, lit up, ringing. Seeing Liam's name on the screen, panic gripped her heart. "Oh my god. What if something happened to Slade at the jump?"

Claire's phone started ringing. She reached for it. "Calm down. Slade's calling me."

"What?" Beyond confused, Savanna answered the call. "Liam?"

"Savanna." His voice boomed in her ear. She pulled the phone a few inches away. "Slade's a good guy. Maybe a little crazy. But he loves you. Please take him back. He's miserable without you. He needs you."

Stunned, she met Claire's gaze. Wide eyed, her friend pointed to her own phone. Slade's voice, a little slurred, came through loud and clear out of the speaker. "Please talk to Liam. He made a mistake today. You guys belong together."

Liam's voice continued to flow out of Savanna's phone. Speech as slurred as Slade's, he reminded her of all of Slade's good points and positive traits. In the background, she could hear Slade's voice as he did the same to Claire. They were obviously sitting together, maybe positioned just as close as she and Claire, clearly drunk, and very sweet for trying to fix each other's relationships.

"He didn't jump," Liam continued. "Realized it was stupid."

"I'm glad." So glad.

"Will you see him?"

Swallowing hard as tears clouded her vision and thickened her throat, she sucked in a breath. "Yes."

"Good." His voice softened. "Have you seen Claire? Is she okay? She shouldn't still be getting so sick. Don't want her ending up in the hospital. Make her see the doctor. Okay?"

"She got a new medicine today and it seems to be keeping the morning sickness at bay."

"Morning sickness?" His voice rose, sharp and loud. "She's pregnant?"

"Um, yeah. You must be pretty drunk if you forgot about the baby." Amused, she rolled her eyes at Claire.

But Claire's face paled. "Wait—"

"Savanna?" Liam's volume increased. "I'm having a baby?"

Savanna's mouth dropped open. Uh oh. "Maybe I'd better put Claire on the phone."

She passed the phone to her stricken friend. "I'm so sorry. But it's been over a week. I thought you told him already."

"No." Taking a deep breath, Claire pulled the phone to her ear. "Liam, I'm here… We're having a baby. I'm… We… We need to talk."

Something banged on his end, followed by a crash as he stumbled around, yelling to Slade, "I need to go, to find Claire."

Slade's voice echoed from both Claire's phone and Savanna's. "We can't drive, Li. I'm seeing two of you. Let's call a car service. Or Dom. He'll take us. Where is she?"

Savanna glanced at the clock and then grabbed her phone. "Liam. It's one-thirty in the morning. Too late to bother Dom. And you guys are too drunk to be roaming around. Claire is with me. She's fine. Go to sleep and sober up. We'll come by and see you tomorrow, okay?"

"What if she needs something tonight?"

"I'll stay with her."

"Okay. Thank you."

"Goodnight." She ended the call and rubbed her hands over her face, torn between laughing and crying.

Beside her, Claire picked up her phone. "Slade? I'm hanging up now. I'll see you—"

"Wait. Make sure Savanna comes tomorrow too." His voice was enough to start Savanna's tears.

"I will." She set her phone aside. "Wow."

"Yeah." Savanna cringed through a guilty grin. "I'm so sorry I spilled the beans."

"It's all right. I really should have told him. I just didn't know how. But I'm glad that he knows. It'll make tomorrow's conversation easier."

"On that note, we should get some sleep."

"The couch pulls out into a bed. And I have pretty much everything you'll need in the bathroom." Claire stood and set her soda in the kitchen.

After Savanna settled on the couch for the night, she lay awake for a long time. Thoughts of Slade, their conversations and experiences, played through her mind.

She had a big decision to make. And morning would arrive far too early.

CHAPTER TWENTY ONE
LIAM

Moving slowly to calm his aching head, Liam refilled his water glass, then joined Slade at the counter. "Morning. Ugh. I'd offer to make breakfast, but I can't even think about food right now. I'll hold off until lunch."

"Same," Slade agreed, eyes as bloodshot as Liam knew his to be. His friend alternated between gulping down a giant glass of water and sipping a small cup of coffee. "I'll count the two aspirin I downed as breakfast."

Liam glanced at his phone, hoping for a text from Claire. Nothing. Whenever she arrived, he would be ready.

He'd showered. Shaved. And ordered three books on pregnancy, parenting, and early childhood development. One of his friends needed to hurry up and have a kid soon so he'd have someone to ask about all things baby-related.

The intercom sounded an hour later as he finished his third glass of water. Feeling clear-headed, he pressed the button. "Yes?"

"It's Claire and Savanna."

"Come on up." Nervous and excited to see Claire, he waited by the door.

Slade wandered over, looking caught between worry and hope. "Good luck."

"You too."

The knock still managed to startle him. He swung the door open. As soon as he met Claire's blue eyes, he all but melted into the floor. How could he stay angry at her? He loved her and now they were having a child. He stepped back to allow them to enter.

Slade and Savanna were staring at each other like they expected the other to disappear. Slade rubbed his hand over the back of his neck. "We can go in my room and talk."

Savanna nodded and followed him down the hall. His door closed a moment later.

Liam closed the front door. All the drama about the job paled in comparison to Claire carrying his child. She still looked too tired. "Are you okay? Still getting sick?"

"The new vitamins I started taking yesterday seem to be working. I got sick once yesterday and once this morning, but I'll take that over the five times a day awfulness I had before. My doctor said about half of the women who get nausea during pregnancy feel complete relief around fourteen weeks. For most others, it takes another month or so for the queasiness to ease up, though it may return later and come and go throughout pregnancy. And a small percentage of women have symptoms that persist continually until delivery."

"I hope you don't have it for that long."

"Me either." Her lips curved in a careful smile. "The ginger ale you bought helps, so thank you."

"Then I'll buy it by the truck full." They were still in the entryway. "Do you need some? I have it here."

She laid her hand on her stomach. "I'm fine. But, thanks."

The urge to touch her there was so strong. He wanted to

place his hand alongside of hers and be close to the place where his child grew. "Come into the living room."

She sat on the end of the couch. He sat half-on the middle and half on the opposite end's cushions, close but not closer than they were ready for. She linked her fingers together, then pulled them apart, then brought one leg up to rest on the cushion and shifted to face him. "We need to talk."

"We do."

"This pregnancy has terrified me. I was so sick I couldn't do my job. I didn't know if any of the medicines were going to work. When Ray approached me, I didn't feel like I could tell him no. If he saw me as uncooperative or not a team player, there's nothing to stop him from replacing me too. I couldn't risk that happening now, not with the baby."

"I understand." He did. He really did.

She reached toward him and then hesitated and returned her hand to her lap. "The thought of being involved in lining up your replacement made me physically sick. I threw up twice that night. I know losing the job would devastate you. I told Ray that too. I couldn't stand having any part in hurting you."

He nodded. Hearing that helped.

"I didn't know how to tell you about it. And I didn't know how to tell you about the baby either. There never was a perfect time. We've only been seeing each other a few months and this pregnancy is a shock."

"It is. We were always so careful. I've wracked my brain trying to remember if we'd ever forgotten to use a condom. But to be honest, I was always so lost in my head over you that I don't think I would've realized if one had broken."

"Worrying about the how doesn't help now. But I'm surprised you haven't made any jokes about your sperm having shark strength or something about them being stealth swimmers." She offered him a hopeful smile.

Laughing, he shifted closer, relieved they could laugh and that she didn't hate him for his hand in the major change in their lives. "You know how my mind works. Believe me, the jokes are forming fast, but I've held back because I wasn't sure if you'd find them funny."

"It's laugh or cry. And I've done my share of crying."

"How long have you known?" He wasn't angry she hadn't told him or that she'd told Savanna first, only curious.

"I found out the day you sprained your ankle."

Rubbing his hand over his forehead, he shook his head. "Talk about timing."

"Listen, Liam…" Pausing, she bit her lip. Eyes wide, she watched him as nerves played over her face.

He couldn't have her worried. Shifting closer, he covered her hand with his. "I'm going to be here for you and the baby every step of the way. We're in this together."

"Together?" Her gaze searched his and she leaned closer but stopped before any other parts of their bodies connected.

"I didn't react well yesterday. There was too much emotion. I should have stayed and talked it out. And I definitely shouldn't have said what I did about us. It isn't true. We're not over. We can't be, not when I love you like I do."

Her eyes welled with tears. She closed the distance, wrapping her other arm around his shoulders. "I love you too."

His lips found hers and he felt the love flowing between them. He shifted their hands to her stomach and thrilled at the idea their baby was right there.

After long moments, Claire drew back. "We still haven't solved the problem of what to do about work. Tomorrow's game will be a test to see how well the medicine works over the smell of the ballpark food. If I can't get a handle on this nausea, I won't be able to do the job. And I honestly don't want to work with another Fin. You're what makes Fin the lovable, dynamic character that he is. Maybe we need to remind Ray of that."

"We can adjust our timing on the field to accommodate whatever breaks you need to take until you're feeling better. The team doesn't have to know about the baby unless you want to tell them."

"Thank you."

"When *are* we having him or her?"

"Mid-February."

"I can't believe we're actually having a kid." He loved the idea. Maybe the baby would be the next in line for Fin or Fiona. That was the only replacement he'd accept. He pulled his laptop from the coffee table. "Let's get Ray on video chat. Settle this now."

She leaned her head on his shoulder as they waited for Ray to accept the call. Liam's fingers stroked over her shoulder.

Finally, Ray's face popped up on the screen. "Oh. Liam *and* Claire. What's going on, guys?"

Liam started right in. "We need to talk to you about the mascot situation."

"What about it?"

"As I continue to heal, I'll be more mobile. I'll be able to dance on top of the dugout. Jog around. Do light stunts on the ATV. So even if I'm not doing flips in three weeks, it'll be a lot better than things have been."

"Liam, the backup is a backup plan. I explained that to you yesterday."

"I respect that, Ray. But I made Fin into the character that the fans love. Not some other guy. Me. No one else has my personality or drive. No one else is as committed to taking

Fin as far as he can go, not only at the ballpark but with the kids in the charity and at Children's Hospital. I work my ass off, during baseball season and in the off-season. I don't think you'll find that kind of commitment with anyone else. No one wants it like I do."

Claire squeezed his hand. "I can't pick someone else over Liam. No one else is Fin to me. He's the reason Fin and Fiona have such chemistry. It's real. That can't be faked with someone else."

Ray regarded them coolly. "So you're telling me that you're involved with each other."

"More than that." Claire glanced at Liam and brought their joined hands to her stomach. If she was ready to tell Ray about their news, he'd fully support her. When he nodded, she returned her focus to the screen. "We're having a baby."

Ray's eyebrows shot up his forehead. "Oh."

"I've been having some nausea that's been difficult to control but otherwise, my doctor said I can continue to do the gymnastics through the end of the season."

"Well, that's good. Your health comes first, but if she gave the approval, that's great."

Liam adjusted his seat on the couch, rocking the laptop so Ray's face blurred. "We're hoping to incorporate more into the Fin and Fiona storyline. If you look at the comments on the site, the fans love us. We can take it to the next level and get them involved. Run a contest where they'll get to appear in the next video with us. Have them help Fin plan a proposal, and vote on everything for the wedding which will take place during the last game of the regular season. It'll be a huge build up. I think we'd get a sellout crowd for Fin and Fiona alone, regardless of who the Riptide are playing on September thirtieth."

Ray ran a pen back and forth between his fingers. He was

quiet for several moments and his face remained impassive. But then he nodded. "I can see how much this means to you both. You're right, Liam, you are the reason Fin is so popular. We do owe you for that. I give you my word. I won't hire anyone else for the rest of the season."

"Thank you." The tension in Liam's muscles released and the web of restraints around his heart broke. At last, he felt more like his old confident self.

"But if by some reason, you're not back to normal by next season's Spring Training, I'll have to look for a new Fin."

"I understand." He did. He totally did. But that wasn't going to be an issue. He'd make sure of it. "But I'll be back for sure. Opening Day is when we'll introduce the world to Fin and Fiona's baby shark."

Ray smiled. "That would be a great start to the new season. All right, you two, you have a deal."

Grinning, Liam tugged Claire to his chest. "Thank you."

Ray signed off and the screen went dark. Liam pulled Claire onto his lap. "We did it."

"I'm so happy he said yes."

"He's not stupid. I think he's already picturing the ticket sales and the merchandise opportunities for Baby Finley."

"Baby Finley?" Face beaming with her smile, Claire wound her arms around his neck. "I like it. And I love you."

He held on tight. "I love you too. What do you think about making Fin and Fiona's wedding coincide with our own?"

"Our own?" She pulled back. "You're asking me to marry you for real?"

"Will you? I don't have a ring but we can pick one out together. I want to spend the rest of my life with you."

Fresh tears sparkled in her eyes and she nodded. "Yes. I

love you so much. I can't wait to marry you. We should do it on the same day as Fin and Fiona."

Happiness surged through him, but he kept his voice fairly even. "You want to get married on a baseball field, in front of thirty thousand people, dressed in a shark costume?"

Laughing, she brushed her hand through his hair. "We can leave the costumes and the crowd for Fin and Fiona. But I do want to marry you on the field where we first met, with our friends and families around us."

"I can't imagine a better way to begin our life together." He kissed her and then tapped her hip. "Let's take this someplace a little more private."

She sent him a teasing smile. "The balcony?"

Chuckling, he drew her to the hall. "The bedroom."

Slade

He closed his bedroom door and watched Savanna cross to the window. Sunlight spotlighted her flowing hair, gold jewelry, and teal dress, she appeared part goddess, part enchantress. He perched on the edge of the bed, grateful for the chance to talk, desperate to somehow win her back, but at a loss as to how to begin.

She tucked her hair behind her ear and licked her lips. "I heard you didn't jump last night."

"Dom and Adam told me that I was being an idiot, but seeing Liam, ready to jump because I needed him and because he thought he'd lost everything, made me realize that it was a dangerous and unwise idea. I couldn't let him jeopardize his recovery. Seeing how my decisions, my actions could potentially hurt someone I love made me change my mind.

See what everyone around me could see. If I can do it for Liam, I can do it for you."

She sighed and shook her head. "Slade."

"You said you didn't want me to do it, that it was danger-ous, and that it really worried you. I was reeling from a lot of emotions last night, so I wasn't thinking clearly. I made a huge mistake in how I handled the whole BASE jumping thing with you. You were right. I should have stopped, then sat down and talked to you about it, like we've always done on anything we've tried. I'm sorry I messed that up—royally. Please don't think that your feelings don't matter to me. They've always mattered."

"But you said you can't stop doing what you love just because I'm uncomfortable."

"I honestly don't know if I can give up skydiving or the other things I like, but I'm willing to try if you'll give us another chance."

Pursing her lips, she shook her head again. "I don't want you resenting me. And I don't want you to change. I'm not saying give them up completely, but if I have what I feel is a legitimate concern about something you want to do, I want to feel like my voice is being heard."

He stood, eager to hold her. "I promise I can do that."

"But still, we're so different. You're adventurous and I'm cautious. You're fearless and I'm so not."

"We balance each other out. And we're not that different, not on what really matters." He crossed to her, slow footsteps, but he was ready to crawl if he needed. "I've gotten you to try some new things and you've filled an emptiness that's been inside me my whole life. When I left Tiffany yesterday, I came to you because my heart knew what it needed. The guys have said they've seen a difference in me. That's you."

"You're going to make me cry."

"I'd like it better if you kissed me instead." He traced a fingertip down her face.

She captured his hand. "Wait. Let me say something. You know I'm a champion worrier. I can't promise that I won't ever worry about the things that made me run scared and end the best relationship I've ever had, but I'll keep trying to get better. I fell in love with you just as you are. There's something special between us. Being without you hurts too much. I can deal with any amount of worrying as long as I have you."

He clasped his other hand to her hip and drew her against him. As soon as their bodies lined up, he felt complete. All his apprehension, all his anxiety let go. This was right. Just this. "Being with you is a rush all on its own. And it's the only one I'm addicted to."

She kissed his palm and pulled him closer. Her hand slid to his neck and she held him tight as he brought their lips together. He angled his mouth and she followed. He deepened the kiss, savoring her taste and the feel of her body against his. If he could go on kissing her forever, he'd be a happy man.

Too soon, she leaned back. Smiling, she traced her fingers over his cheek. "I love you, Slade. You're the only one for me."

I love you.

The words stamped themselves across his heart. His eyes burned and tears formed colorful prisms in his eyes. A few spilled over when he blinked them back, and Savanna brushed them away. "I never heard that growing up. Never until Dom, Adam, and Liam. Up until now, they're the only ones I've said that to. But I've wanted to say it to you for weeks. I love you, Savanna. More than I thought I could love anyone."

Her eyes watered. She sniffed and laughed while he

wiped them away. And then he went back to kissing her. They held each other in the beam of sunshine, soaking in the warmth of their love.

A few hours later, he and Savanna arrived at Tiffany and James' house. Talking with Liam well into the night, and then Savanna that morning had helped him see more clearly and objectively. He didn't blame Tiffany. He couldn't. Life hadn't been kind to her either. Her actions had been based in love.

Tiffany led them into the sun room and chose the chair, leaving them the couch. She smoothed her skirt and then cleared her throat. "Thank you for coming back. I've been thinking so much about what you told me. I'm so sorry for all you went through. I wasn't strong enough at twenty-two to fight for you and I've always regretted it. Can you ever forgive me?"

Holding Savanna's hand, he squeezed and waited for the reassuring press of soft fingers. "There's nothing to forgive. I'm sure it wasn't easy for you. I had time to think too. I'm glad you got away from your abuser. I didn't like thinking about you and Melanie and the kids being in that environment."

Smiling, she folded her fidgeting hands on her lap. "Thank you. It took me a long time. I didn't leave until I was thirty. I used to wish that life had turned out differently, but if it had, I might not have Melanie, Chloe or Caden."

He wouldn't wish any of them away. "If life had worked out differently, then maybe I wouldn't have ended up playing baseball, or meeting Liam, Dom, and Adam. I wouldn't have met Savanna. And I can't imagine my life without them. I think life worked out the way it was supposed to."

Tiffany wiped her eyes. "I found James again after all those years. And we found you. You have no idea how happy I am that we found you."

"It's a fresh start for everyone." He embraced Tiffany. The past was in the past. He was ready to focus on the future.

Texts from Dom, Adam, and Liam had fired up his phone during the visit with Tiffany. He passed it to Savanna when they were on their way home. "What's going on with the crew?"

"They're all asking how you are, how the visit went, and the last from Liam was that everyone is in your apartment, so we should meet them there."

He grinned. "I like having a full house."

"I know you do." She reached over the console and patted his thigh then let her hand rest there.

They walked into the apartment and a chorus of greetings tumbled together along with two distinctive barks that meant Dom and Adam had brought their dogs.

Slade stepped halfway in front of Savanna, ready to intercept the huge beasts. They barreled into him, jumping up, licking, barking, and then sniffing Savanna. She laughed and stroked their heads. He kept his arm around her as they moved to the kitchen. Liam and Claire sat together at the counter. Dom and Adam and their wives leaned against the opposite side. Slade pulled up a stool at the end for Savanna. "Whoa, full house tonight."

Liam grinned. "Lots to celebrate. I'm cleared to return to PT next week. Ray promised that Claire and I have full run of the mascot entertainment for the rest of the season, and I get to watch the dogs again during team road trips." Then he wrapped his arm around Claire. "And, the best news, Claire and I are engaged."

Cheers echoed through the room as hugs and well wishes were exchanged.

Slade moved through the kitchen as six different conversations resumed all at once. He grabbed drinks for Savanna and himself.

Dom pulled him aside after he set them on the table. "You okay?"

"I am. Really. Everything is good with Tiffany."

"I'm glad. And Savanna? You guys worked things out?"

"We did." He couldn't stop his smile. "She loves me."

Dom clapped him on the shoulder. "Of course she does. I'm proud of you, Slade. You had a lot thrown at you this season and you handled it all like a champ."

Happiness swelled until Slade nearly burst with it. "I might have had a little help from my friends. Okay, a lot of help. Thanks for always looking out for me."

"Anytime, bud. Anytime."

They rejoined their friends. He slipped his arm around Savanna, and she turned and smiled and leaned against his side.

Love had been his salvation. Savanna had come into his life and changed him in ways he hadn't expected. And loving her was far more exhilarating than any adventure he'd ever known.

With her and his friends by his side, there wasn't any challenge they couldn't handle together.

CHAPTER TWENTY TWO

LIAM

From his position at home plate, Liam adjusted the head of his shark costume and made a last-minute check of Fin's tuxedo. The wedding was about to begin in front of a sold out crowd. Per the Fin and Fiona videos, they had only a few minutes of air time between the sixth and seventh innings. Luckily, the Riptide were winning, but the majority of the crowd were already cheering Fin and Fiona's names. The team would be moving on to the playoffs, but the celebration for this final game in the regular season was all about the mascots' wedding.

All the Riptide players lined up along the dugout. Dom, Adam, and Slade stood closest to him. They'd played starring roles in Fin and Fiona's antics over the course of their relationship. The fans had voted for Dom to preside over the ceremony.

The bridal march echoed through the stadium. Liam turned toward the visitors' dugout. Nurse Fiona emerged, wearing a white dress and veil instead of her blue scrubs. She walked on a white runner covered with the fans' choice of red and pink rose petals.

Liam watched the crowd's reaction. Fiona was as loved as Fin. When she reached him, he raised his hands to his heart.

Dom joined them, holding a microphone. "Riptide fans, we've watched Fin and Fiona fall in love this season, and through your help, they've arrived at this special day. Fin, do you take Fiona to be your wife?"

Liam gave an exaggerated and vehement nod and the crowd cheered.

"And Fiona, do you take Fin to be your husband?"

She nodded and with both hands, blew Fin a kiss.

Dom raised his hands. "Then by the power vested in me by the Riptide fandom, I now pronounce you married."

Grasping Claire's hands, Liam leaned down until the mouths of the costumes met. Cheers and applause rang out at deafening levels.

Claire grinned at him through the dark mesh. "Love you. Can't wait to do this for real later."

"Me either." He squeezed her hands once more, then let go. "Ready. On three. One. Two. Three. Go."

He crouched and then leapt high, throwing his body backward. Blue sky and then the green grass filled his vision and he grinned as he and Claire stuck the landings perfectly and simultaneously.

The crowd roared over their tandem backflip. They waved to the crowd and then he grabbed her hand and they ran to their waiting golf cart, decorated with streamers and crepe paper bells and a *Just Married* sign on the back. He hopped inside, made sure Claire was securely next to him, and then he shot off across the field, toward the tunnel, as the fans cheered around them.

Long after the game ended, when sunset streaked across the sky, Liam again stood at home plate, this time, wearing a dark gray suit, and at Claire's request, a bright blue tie that matched the sash she'd wear on her gown. Nerves pricked his stomach and his heart beat faster. He took a breath and tried to calm down, focusing on the soft strains of the violin music filling the air.

His best man Slade and groomsmen Dom and Adam stood to his left.

Two sections of chairs lined the infield in front of the pitcher's mound. Liam's family on the left and Claire's on the right.

His cousin Hunter and his wife had flown in from New York, bringing more toys to donate to the charity. They sat with Liam's parents, some of the Riptide players, and Adam and Dom's wives. Raymond and Andy were guests too.

Claire's side had her dad and sisters. The sisters' relationship with Claire had improved nearly one hundred percent from when he'd first been introduced to the family. Her dad had attended several Riptide games and had done his best to help them with every baby question they tossed his way.

Love was all around, everywhere he looked.

The violinist switched to a new song. All eyes turned toward the Riptide's dugout. Savanna emerged first, as Claire's maid of honor. She wore a dress of brilliant blue and a smile as wide as the sky when her gaze met Slade's. He offered her his arm and escorted her to her place at the plate.

Claire glided up the dugout steps, a vision in white in a sexy gown, with that bright blue sash at her waist. His mouth went dry. She'd told him it was a mermaid gown. He hadn't a clue what that meant except that if she'd been a sea siren, he'd gladly have jumped overboard.

She kept her gaze on his, her smile trembling, as she came to his side. And then she slipped her hand in his and all was right with his world.

He listened as the officiant spoke of love, then made his vow to love, honor, and cherish Claire forever. He slipped the ring on her finger and couldn't stop smiling.

She repeated the vows, squeezing his hand for emphasis as she spoke in a calm, clear voice. When she slid the ring on his finger, he felt complete.

He drew her into his arms, and bent to kiss her. Claire's lips softened under his and he poured all of the love and promise he felt into the kiss.

The guests cheered and the celebration was underway.

As the night wound down, Liam gathered with Claire and their friends in the dugout for a quiet moment.

Dom handed them an elaborately wrapped box. "Happy wedding. Here you go, from all of us."

Liam set the box on the bench and he and Claire tugged off the wrapping and the lid. Sifting through tissue paper, he spied a shark fin, and lifted it. Not just a fin. But a baby shark costume. His heart swelled with happiness and laughter burst out as it radiated through him. "I love it. It's perfect."

He held up the outfit, then handed it to Claire.

Slade clapped him on the back. "We can't wait for you to introduce the baby to the fans next season. They're going to go crazy."

"Everyone has been rooting for Fin and Fiona." Claire smiled and leaned into Liam's chest.

"Can't go against true love." Liam bent until his lips touched Claire's soft mouth.

She'd been an unexpected surprise. The best thing in his life had come out of the worst experience he'd ever had. He wrapped his arm around her and settled on hand on her stomach. He couldn't wait to meet his child and to share his life with the baby and Claire.

Everything was changing again. He couldn't control what it, but he was ecstatic about it, and all he could see was a future that ended in a happily-ever-after.

Slade

Slade was late. He sped through the hospital's hallways on his way to pick up Savanna so they could visit Claire and Liam in the maternity wing. He hated being late. Especially for Savanna. Especially today. Once again, LA's horrible traffic hadn't cooperated during his drive.

She stood when he entered her office and held out a colorful card. "It's from Mason. He's officially in remission."

He closed the door, then kissed her, and then checked out the *thank you* card. "I'm so happy. I love that kid."

"Me too." Savanna grabbed her purse. "Speaking of kids, we should go."

He linked their hands together. The ring he'd picked up from the jeweler that morning was burning a hole in his pocket. Waiting to propose wasn't an option now that he had her so close to him. "In a second."

Savanna squeezed his hand as she studied his face. "You seem pretty nervous considering this isn't even your child. You're more wound up than Liam when he called to let us know the baby was on its way."

He nodded, even as his heartbeat galloped. "Yeah. There's another reason."

"What's wrong?" She set her purse down and regarded him with wide eyes.

He drew her over to the chairs in front of her desk. "We need to talk."

Her gaze turned cautious and she sank into the seat. "Slade? What's going on?"

"Nothing bad. Just thinking about something I need to do. But I need you to do it with me."

She gave him a half-smile. "I'm still working off the thrill of scuba diving with the dolphins. But lay it on me. What adventure are you looking to do next?"

He had a new contract and a promise to the team to keep his adventurous activities limited to the off-season. He still did them, but that need had lessened a lot since he'd found Savanna. "Nothing like that. Something bigger. Something permanent. Something I'm hoping you'll like."

Her brows arched. "Permanent. Like, matching tattoos?"

He lifted her hand to his lips and pressed a kiss to where his ring would hopefully soon reside. "How about matching rings? Will you marry me?"

Her eyes grew wide and her hand tightened around his. "Yes. Definitely yes."

Relief mixed with joy and he leaned back in the chair, searching his pocket for the ring. Her hand shook as he slid the oval-shaped diamond surrounded by aquamarine stones onto her finger. "It looks good there."

"It belongs there." She slid her hands along his jaw and drew him toward her. Soft tips touched his in slow exploration. He splayed his hand across her back as his body heated with want and need and love.

After a long moment, he lifted his head. "I know you're not crazy about the penthouse. I was thinking we'd buy something new together. There's a property for sale near Dom on a good-sized piece of land with two houses on it. Liam and I were thinking that he and Claire and the baby could live in one and you and I could live in the other. But only if you like it."

He hoped she would. He needed to be close to the family he'd created. "If you don't like it, that's fine. I want to be close to the guys but I'll live anywhere you want. The place doesn't matter as long as you're there. You're home to me."

Her eyes sparkled with tears. "I can't wait to see the house. I know you need the guys. I'd like it if Claire was close by."

"Good. Because we already put a deposit down. We didn't want to lose it." He rubbed his thumb over her knuckle, above her ring, while she laughed. "I can't wait to marry you."

"Me either. I wish we could do it tonight so we could wake up already married tomorrow morning. You're home to me too, you know."

A rush ran through him at her words. "Then let's do it. We can fly to Vegas tonight. As soon as we see the baby."

Biting her lip, she tilted her head to the side, and studied their joined hands. "As much as I want to, I can't not have my parents at our wedding. They won't be back from their trip until next week."

"Right. And I want the guys there. And Tiffany, James, and the kids too." Pitchers and catchers were due to report to Spring Training in six days. He had to head to Arizona the following week. He needed to think. "Getting married during the season will be hard. We'll probably have to wait until November."

"I don't really want to wait that long."

"Then, we won't. As long as you don't mind waiting on the honeymoon. The team has two days off between the end of Spring Training and the start of the season. It's a weekend. We'll get married on that Saturday. It can be as small or large a wedding as you want."

Eyes sparkling, she shifted onto his lap and wrapped her

arms around him. "Our first date was in a hot air balloon. We could rent a big one and have the wedding ceremony there."

"You're willing to recite vows with me at two thousand feet?" He was impressed. She'd continued to impress him on a daily basis with her bravery in trying things that gave her pause and in her ability to ground him when he needed it most.

"It'll be a full circle moment."

"It's perfect." He kissed her again, overwhelmed with love for the woman by his side.

After a phone call to her parents to share their news, they arrived at the maternity wing. Slade knocked on the open door to Claire's private room. "We heard there's a new addition to the Riptide family in here."

Liam grinned and waved them inside. "It's a boy. We have a son."

Slade rounded the bed to Liam's side, hugged him, and studied the tiny bundle sleeping in Claire's arms. "Congratulations."

Liam stroked his finger against his son's cheek, and then his gaze met Slade's. "This is Slade Devereux York."

Slade blinked. "You gave him my name?"

"It's only right that he shares the name of my brother and best friend, and if you're willing, his godfather." Liam smiled. "What do you say?"

"Dude." Swallowing hard, Slade grabbed him in a hard hug. Family. All his life, he'd thought he'd missed out on having one. But he had people he belonged to and who belonged to him. And now, this brand-new, very special bond that would link Liam and him forever. "Saying thank you doesn't seem like enough. But thank you."

Liam patted him on the back and dropped his tone to a

murmur. "Love you, bro. This is proof that you're stuck with me forever."

Chuckling through his tears, Slade pulled back and wiped his eyes. "Good."

"Want to hold the baby?"

"What if I drop him?"

Savanna's chuckle eased his worry. "Isn't that my line?"

"You won't." Liam lifted the baby from Claire and placed him in Slade's arms.

Slade stared at his sleeping namesake and brushed his finger over the baby's tiny hand. "Hey there, little guy."

Little Slade turned his head and then wrapped his hand around Slade's finger in a surprisingly strong grip. Slade couldn't speak over the lump in his throat. He swallowed hard against the hot tears burning again below the surface. Liam's arm draped around his shoulder and he met his gaze. He didn't have the words to describe how he felt or how to tell Liam and Claire how much the gesture meant to him. But Liam seemed to understand.

Beside the bed, Savanna bent to hug Claire. "Congratulations."

"Thank you." She grinned right before nabbing Savanna's wrist. "Don't move so fast. What's on your finger? Is that what I think it is?"

His new fiancée nodded. "But today is about you and Liam and your beautiful bundle of joy."

"It's about all of us." Claire waved her down for another hug. "I'm so happy for you guys."

"That's awesome." Liam clapped Slade on the back and then leaned in, lowering his voice. "Did you ask about the house?"

Savanna's musical laughter lit up Slade's heart. "He did, and I'm happy we'll be next-door neighbors."

Slade passed the baby back to Liam, and then slid his arm around Savanna. She kissed his jaw and wrapped her arms around his waist. Feeling like the luckiest guy in the world, he held on tight.

A short time later, Dom and Adam and their wives came in and the room filled with cheers and congratulations and well wishes for the new family and for Slade and Savanna.

Slade glanced around the room, smiling at the people he loved and would do anything for without question. As a kid, he dreamed about making it to the big leagues, having a family of his own, and someone to love him. People who would never leave.

He had it all. His dream had come true.

Thank you so much for reading *Enamored*! If you enjoyed the book, please consider leaving a review. Reviews, even one-sentence long, help other readers find my books.

Don't miss the other books in the Game of Love series:

Rekindled

Weary of small roles in low-budget films, actress Gemma Norwood isn't sure if her heart still lies in making movies, but giving up would be admitting failure and throwing away her dream. An escape back to her hometown, a snow-covered small town in the Catskills, is the perfect place to contemplate her life. Even if the chances are pretty good that she'll run into the one man who broke her heart. She can handle it. After all, she is an actress.

Winter is the worst season for pro baseball pitcher Adam Hudson. It gives him too much time to think. He may have physically healed from the line-drive that fractured his skull, but emotionally, he has a long way to go. Questioning whether he can continue to play the game he loves leads to questioning everything, including the choice he made that took Gemma away from him.

Coming face to face in nearly the same way they'd originally met, Adam and Gemma can't deny their chemistry is still there, or that they've both kept tabs on each other in the four years since their break-up. But with so much time passed, and emotions unresolved, and things left unsaid, can they start something new, or will old hurts and new fear threaten to strike them out?

Captivated

Domingo Torres, star center fielder for the Los Angeles Riptide, needs to stay off management's radar after a Spring Training game ended in flying fists and bloodshed. He's ordered to keep a lid on his temper and a low profile for the rest of the season. Keeping his focus solely on baseball isn't a problem — until he meets his sexy new neighbor, and his thoughts shift to a lot more than his batting average.

After years of complete control in handling every aspect of her brother's multi-platinum selling rock band, Irisa Rostov is ready to crack. And it doesn't help that the band is on the verge of self-destruction. Playing peacemaker and keeping them together for the last eight weeks of their spring concert series is all that matters, until she meets Dom, and the feelings he stirs up causes the guards around her heart to weaken.

Getting distracted by romance is the last thing Irisa wants, and being in the headlines is the last thing Dom needs, but their attraction is undeniable, their connection is immediate, and staying away is impossible.

Check out the series:

https://www.susanscottshelley.com/gameoflove

ABOUT THE AUTHOR

USA TODAY bestselling author Susan Scott Shelley writes romance with heat and heart that celebrates love without limits. She enjoys watching hockey, training for her next run, reading romance novels, and binging episodes of her favorite British TV shows. Susan lives in Philadelphia with her husband and also works as a professional voice over artist. A city girl who likes being out in nature as often as possible, she has yet to meet a plant she hasn't wanted to take home and she really wants a pet crow.

Visit her at https://susanscottshelley.com.

ALSO BY SUSAN SCOTT SHELLEY

<u>The Games We Play series</u>

Power Move

<u>The Philadelphia Frenzy series</u>

Mad Scramble, Hometown Hero, Team Spirit

<u>The Falling series</u>

Falling Faster

Hold on Forever (related to the series)

<u>Bliss Bakery series</u>

Sugar Crush, Heart of the Batter, Home Made, Sweet Hearts

<u>Pride of the Bedlam series</u>

Skating on Chance, Holding on Tight, Scoring Slater

Playing with Pride (series collection)

<u>Philadelphia Power series</u>

Against the Rush, Over the Top, Behind the Mask, From the First

Powered by Love (series collection)

<u>Love & Rugby series</u>

Spiral, Spark, Smolder, Shine, Surprise, Swoon

Love & Rugby, vol. 1, Love & Rugby, vol. 2,

Love & Rugby, the Complete Collection

Love & Rugby: Season of Love

Savor, Seduce, Stay

Love & Rugby: Season of Love, the Complete Collection

Buffalo Bedlam series

Making His Move, Fighting For More, Taking His Shot

Playing to Win (series collection)

Rocked by Love series

Love Notes, Love Song

Game of Love series

Rekindled, Captivated, Enamored

Game of Love (series collection)

Holiday Hearts series

Kiss Me Again, More Than Words, All I Want, Marry Me

Holiday Hearts (series collection)

Other Novellas

Flirting on Ice, Simmering Ice, Tackled by the Girl Next Door

Sign up for Susan's newsletter:

https://susanscottshelley.com/newsletter